Nasrudin:
the world's

MW01125856

Nasrudin:
the world's best-loved wise fool

Raj Arumugam

Contents

The world's best-loved wise fool

Nasrudin is the world's best-loved fool. *The wise fool.*

Stories about Nasrudin have been told and re-told – and new ones invented – since the Middle Ages.

Most of the stories of Nasrudin appear as jokes – but each story invites deep thought.

Each story offers an insight into life and our very own nature.

Nasrudin lived some time in the thirteenth century and is claimed by so many nations of the Near, Middle East and Central Asia as their own.

Today, Nasrudin has many websites devoted to him – and he has truly become the world's best loved fool. *Ooops! - the world's best-loved wise fool…*

Raj Arumugam,   January 2010

Prologue:
Remembering Nasrudin

Prologue: Remembering Nasrudin

You ask if I knew Nasrudin.
You have heard the news, have you?
Just days ago, just days ago – Nasrudin passed away.
You have heard the news, and you see me in a pensive
mood, and you ask if I knew Nasrudin.

Well, to ask if I knew Nasrudin is to ask if I know
myself.
For Nasrudin and I were once neighbors and the closest
of friends.
My friend and companion, Nasrudin.

We grew up in the same village and we studied at the
same schools when our families moved to the town and
then to the city.
I was the indoor type, shy and devoted to my studies; but
Nasrudin loved the outdoors and the woods and the
streets. Still we were good friends.

Ah, yes, Nasrudin and I were the best of friends…

I loved to hear Nasrudin talk. I loved his voice and his
company. Why? Because when he spoke with me, I
realized there was something in his words that I could
never get from the books. Because his voice rang with a
certain vision, something that plunged into the depths of
my mind. Often did I visit him when he was home, and
I questioned him, and listened to him.

But then we separated…I moved far away to the Grand City, and he continued living in the town where he and I had studied… Yes, he did move about and he traveled – but most of his life he spent in his town and in his village…

Ah, yes, my dear friend Nasrudin is dead….
And you ask if I knew Nasrudin.

You ask if he were a madman as some think he was...you ask if he was a fool….or mystic...or saint…*what was he?* – you ask…I certainly knew him – but you must decide what he was…You must decide what he is to you… And yes, I will tell you stories of this man…I will tell the stories of this man whom some call fool and yet some call wise…
I will narrate, as I remember, some of the stories I know of Nasrudin…and you decide what he is to you….

Ah, I remember many things about Nasrudin… I remember as if they happen right here before my eyes…some events appear as if they are in the distant past – and yet some as if happening even now, right before my very eyes…

Come, let us sit below this tree and I shall tell you these stories as they come to me...
I shall tell you these stories as I remember them, and as they are...in no particular order, in no particular sequence – but certainly as faithfully as I can...

And then you decide for yourself, you decide if he was a madman or a fool; or a mystic or a wise fool...listen and decide...

And there was one such occasion...I see it as if it is happening right here and now...

The Nasrudin stories

Ah, I remember many things about Nasrudin... I remember as if they happen right here before my eyes...some events appear as if they are in the distant past – and yet some as if happening even now, right before my very eyes...

Nasrudin: duck soup

1

Poor Nasrudin.
For many days he has had the desire for duck soup – but he has no money to buy any.

But today he is determined to have duck soup at any cost.

He must have duck soup with his bread today. He must. In fact, he is going mad with this desire for duck soup…

He will have duck soup! *Duck soup! Duck soup! Quack! Quack! Quack! Duck soup! Duck soup! Quack! Quack! Quack!*

2
So he rides to the town park.
It is a beautiful park and there are groups of people here and there, enjoying the evening.
He ties his donkey to a tree near the edge of the lake.

Nasrudin sits on the grass. He has brought a bag of bread and he breaks the bread, and throws bits of bread crumbs to the ducks.
The ducks swiftly pluck the bread crumbs out of the ground - and they fly away from Nasrudin just as swiftly.

Hmmm, moans Nasrudin. *I don't think I can catch any. Dead ducks are too expensive and live ducks are too fast for me! I give up!*

But, truly, Nasrudin is not the sort who gives up.
He waves to his donkey and he goes to the lake. He stands in the lake with the water to his knees.
He dips bits of his bread in the water and he eats the wet bread.

Nasrudin! shouts a group of children who are playing at the edge of the lake. *What are you doing?*
Yes, what are you doing? shouts a woman.

Can't you see? shouts back Nasrudin. *Can't you see I'm having bread with my duck soup?!*

Hee-haw! Hee-haw! says the donkey.

When the lie becomes the truth

Nasrudin was quite a trickster when he was young.
He and his friends were often idle and sat in a corner of
the city square and loved playing tricks on people.
And there was one such occasion…this I see it as if it is
happening right here and now…

1

Ah, Nasrudin and his friend are sitting in a corner of the
town square.
Nasrudin's donkey stands just beside him.
Nasrudin, says the friend.
What, dear friend? says Nasrudin.
Hee-haw? says the donkey, eager to participate in any
adventure.
There are so many people today, says the friend.
Hee-haw, brays the donkey, rather disappointed at this
rather insipid observation of the obvious.

It's time for a trick! says Nasrudin.
Hee-haw! Hee-haw! brays the donkey, truly appreciative
of the genius of its master.

2

Ladies and gentlemen! shouts Nasrudin. He jumps atop his donkey and rides quickly into the middle of the square and he shouts again: *Ladies and gentlemen!* *Hee-haw! Hee-haw!* brays the donkey, looking as dignified as possible.

And Nasrudin's friend runs forward and stands beside Nasrudin and the donkey.
Ladies and gentlemen! shouts Nasrudin again.
The crowd is silent.
The people are still. They look at Nasrudin and his donkey and Nasrudin's friend with eager expectation.

Hee-haw! Hee-haw! brays the donkey, announcing its approval.

3

Ladies and gentlemen, says Nasrudin. *My friend here who stands before me has made a great discovery.* And the crowd focuses its attention on Nasrudin's friend.

Hee-haw! hee-haw! brays the donkey, trying to shift attention back to itself.

Ladies and gentlemen, continues Nasrudin, *my friend has discovered gold!*
Yes! Yes! shouts the friend.
Hee-haw! Hee-haw! brays the donkey.

15

Gold? Gold? Where? Where? shouts the crowd.

And Nasrudin continues :
It is true. My friend has just discovered chests of gold
buried perhaps hundreds of years before but now
exposed after the rains we've had these many days!
Gold!
Chests of gold! - my dear people!

Gold! Gold! shout the people.
Hee-haw!Hee-haw! brays the donkey.

Nasrudin's friend stands amazed and silent.

Where? Where? shout the people.
Hee-haw! Hee-haw! echoes the donkey.

And Nasrudin declares:
Dearest people – my friend was walking in the fields just
beyond the town square, and there right in the eastern
corner of the open fields are these chests of gold all now
exposed because of the heavy rains we've had! In the
eastern corner of the fields, my people!

And suddenly the crowd goes berserk. *Gold! Gold!* They
scream and they abandon their shops and their activities,
and they rush towards the fields. It's each man and
woman for themselves! *Gold ! Gold!* scream the people -
and they push and jostle and run out of the square –
leaving Nasrudin, his donkey and Nasrudin's friend in
the square.

Suddenly Nasrudin rides his donkey in the direction of the fields.

Where are you going, Nasrudin? shouts the friend, running behind Nasrudin and his donkey.

I'm going for the gold too! shouts Nasrudin.
Hee-haw! Hee-haw! brays the donkey excitedly.

Gold? Gold? shouts the friend. *But, Nasrudin - it's a trick. It's a lie to trick the crowd.*

You fool! shouts Nasrudin, still riding towards the fields. *Can't you see that so many people believe in it? – and therefore it must be true!*
Hee-haw! Hee-haw! brays the donkey excitedly, carrying its master towards the fields and the gold - as quickly as it can. *Hee-haw! Hee-haw!*

Ah, those were the days when the world was young and Nasrudin and his friends played their tricks on the people of the city...

Mankind's best qualities

Nasrudin, a visiting philosopher, and Nasrudin's donkey
sit in the shade under a tree.
The visiting philosopher is a world-renowned
philosopher, and also known famously as the
Philosopher with the Thousand Questions.

What are the two best qualities of mankind, Nasrudin?
asks the visiting philosopher.

Hee-haw! says the donkey, though its opinion was not
asked for.

There are two, says Nasrudin.

And what are the two? asks the philosopher.

Hee-haw! Hee-haw! says the donkey.

Sssssh! says the philosopher, waving his right hand
rather impatiently at the donkey. And then he turns to
Nasrudin and says: *Please answer me, Nasrudin.*

Hee-haw! hee-haw! says the donkey.

And Nasrudin says: *My father only told me one of the
two for he had forgotten one.*

And the philosopher glares at the donkey, trying to frighten it into silence, and he looks at Nasrudin, and he asks:
So which one of the two of the best qualities of humanity did your father remember and tell you?

Hee-haw! says the donkey.

And Nasrudin says: *To tell you the truth, just as he forgot one of the two, I've forgotten the one he told me…And so it's all lost in time…*

Hee-haw! Hee-haw! says the donkey.

And the philosopher stares at the donkey and then looks at Nasrudin, and he takes his leave, completely perplexed, and none the wiser than when he arrived.

A job for Nasrudin

1

Young Nasrudin was rather lazy. He spent much of his time talking to his friends in the streets, telling them stories, and making fun of the proud and vain and those dressed in expensive clothes.

Come and work in my shop, said Nasrudin's father to Nasrudin.

Yes, Father. But you may find a decline in your business if I worked for you, said Nasrudin quickly.

How is that? asked Nasrudin's father.

Well, being your son and therefore being extremely clever, you'll find that I will outshine all your staff. Then you'll find you'll have to promote me – and then the other staff may be jealous and de-motivated, thinking I was promoted for being your son and not for my brilliance in business – and once staff are de-motivated, as you know, they will not work well and so your business will suffer, and so it is best that I do not work for you.

Very well then, said Nasrudin's father, with a cunning smile. *You'll work in my friend's granary stacking sacks of grain. There you won't have to use your brains – just your muscles!*

2

And so Nasrudin's father outwitted Nasrudin and got
him to work in his friend's granary.
It was hard work.
The workers rushed from street to the storehouse or from
the storehouse to the street where the carts waited. Each
worker carried on his back at least two sacks at a time.

But Nasrudin only carried one sack at a time.

The foreman was quite unhappy and he called Nasrudin
into his office.

Nasrudin, said the foreman.
Yes, Sir, said Nasrudin.
*You know you are not to have any privileges here
because your father is a friend of the granary's owner,*
said the foreman.
Yes Sir, said Nasrudin. *In fact, Sir, I do not want any
privileges anywhere.*
Then why is it, asked the foreman, *that it takes you two
trips to carry two sacks when everyone else can carry
two sacks on one trip?*
Oh Sir, said Nasrudin, *as you can see, they are all just
too darned lazy to make two trips! I'm not afraid to
make two trips, Sir!*

3

That evening, Nasrudin's father came home quite displeased.

Nasrudin! shouted Nasrudin's father.
Yes, Father? asked Nasrudin.
I heard you lost your job? said Nasrudin's father. *Tell me what happened.*

Nasrudin explained what happened and then he said: *It is better that way, Father.*

How's that? asked Nasrudin's father.

It is better that one does not work in a place where they sack people for being clever and reward people for being silly! Father – such a business will sack itself soon enough! said Nasrudin.

Dear son, said Nasrudin's father.
Yes, Father? said Nasrudin.
You are going to have a difficult life, said the father.
How's that? asked Nasrudin.

Because, dear son, you are too clever for most and most are too foolish for you. There is no work for such people, Nasrudin.

Perhaps, said Nasrudin, with a grin to console his father *– perhaps it might all work out if I could be everybody's fool?*

Past and future

Nasrudin sits drinking tea at the town inn.
Nasrudin sighs often and looks quite sad.

A man at the next table notices how sad Nasrudin looks
and says to him:
Nasrudin...my dear friend...why do you look so sad?

Nasrudin looks up at the man and he says:
*Ah, my dear friend...I am sad as I think about my
future....and my future does not look too good...*

Nasrudin's friend nods and he says:
But what makes your future look so bleak?

My past, dear friend, says Nasrudin. *My past makes my
future look bleak.*

But, says the friend, *should we really worry about the
past? Live this moment, the present!*

Oh, indeed? asks Nasrudin. *Living carelessly thus, that's
how my present rolled on and thus that's how my past
got bad!*

Right shoe first

Nasrudin's wife noticed how Nasrudin always put his right shoe on first - and only then his left shoe. Nasrudin never put on his left shoe first.

One day, Nasrudin's wife decided to ask her husband about this peculiar habit.

Nasrudin, she said. *I have never seen you put your left shoe on first. Why do you always put your right shoe on first?*

Why do I put on my right shoe first? Well, said Nasrudin *– wouldn't it be absolutely silly of me to put my wrong shoe on first? Then both shoes will be wrong! For if I had the wrong shoe on one foot to begin with, then I'd have the wrong shoes on both feet! But if I start with the right shoe, then I'll get it right on both feet!*

Turban of learning

It was evening. Nasrudin sat in the shade of a tree just outside his house. His donkey sat beside him, observing people returning home from their fields or from the town centre.

Hey Nasrudin! shouted a neighbor, walking towards Nasrudin.
The donkey was startled out of its reverie and jumped up, and brayed anxiously:
Hee-haw! Hee-haw!
Lie down donkey, said Nasrudin. *Lie down. It's just Loud and Noisy Abdul.*
Nasrudin's donkey settled down again on the ground in the shade.

Hey Nasrudin! shouted the man again, now standing beside Nasrudin.
Hi Abdul, said Nasrudin.

And Abdul said: *Nasrudin, I have a letter from the Mayor of the neighboring town and I need you to read it out to me. Ah, indeed it is a privilege to have a neighbor like you who knows how to read. Indeed, Nasrudin, the turban is truly a sign of your learning. The turban has magic!*

Donkey looked up at Loud and Noisy Abdul.
And Nasrudin smiled and reached out to receive the letter that Abdul was holding out in his right hand.

Nasrudin looked at the letter but found that it was in a script he had never learned to read.

I am sorry, said Nasrudin to Loud And Noisy Abdul. *I am sorry, Abdul. I can't read that letter as it is in a script I have never learned to read.*
And Nasrudin handed the letter back to Abdul.

And Abdul shouted at Nasrudin:
What kind of a learned man are you, Nasrudin? A turban is a sign of learning and has magical power. You should return that turban to the authorities for if you can't read a letter that turban should not be on your head!

Nasrudin took off his turban immediately and put it on Abduls' head.
All right, said Nasrudin – *if you think that turban truly has such power why don't you read that letter – now that the turban is on your head?*

And the donkey rolled over in the sand and brayed: *Hee-haw! Hee-haw!*

Nasrudin: half the request

Nasrudin was at an inn on the other side of town. He sat at a table drinking a cup of tea.

Suddenly a friend of Nasrudin sat down in the chair before Nasrudin and said:
Ah dear friend, Nasrudin. It's been long since I last saw you.
Yes, said Nasrudin, nervously.

Would you my dear friend, said Nasrudin's friend, *lend me a 100 silver coins for three months?*

And Nasrudin said: *Ah, my dear friend. Sadly, I can fulfill only half your request.*

And the friend smiled and said: *Well, that's all right Nasrudin. I'm sure I can borrow the other 50 silver coins from somebody else.*

Oh no! said Nasrudin. *Half your request was for three months which I can certainly lend: but you'll still have to borrow the 100 silver coins from somebody else!*

Nasrudin: group prayer

If a hundred of us sit together and each prays for one's needs aloud, and the other ninety-nine sing out aloud: O Almighty, make true my neighbor's prayer - then each prayer will come true.

-    Holy Man of the Imperial and Everlasting City,
     visiting Nasrudin's town in the fortieth year of
Nasrudin's life

And so a hundred men are gathered in the Town Hall of the town where Nasrudin lives, and all hundred sit round the Town Hall table.

A silence descends on the gathering there, and the first man says aloud his prayer:
O Almighty, let me have a thousand gold coins by the end of the day!
And the rest of the gathering immediately sings out:
O Almighty, let his prayer be answered.

Another man prays aloud: *O Almighty, let me have a thousand acres of land by the end of the year!*
And the rest of the gathering immediately sings out:
O Almighty, let his prayer be answered.

And so each man prays, each saying aloud his heart's wish and asking that the Almighty grant his prayer – and each time the gathering sings out aloud: *O Almighty, let his prayer be answered.*

And then when over four scores of men have prayed aloud, and the gathering has sung out aloud after each prayer: *O Almighty, let his prayer be answered* – it is now Nasrudin's turn to say aloud his heart's desire.

And Nasrudin says aloud:
O Almighty, each prayer that each man has uttered and that each will utter until all hundred gathered here are done – may each and every good thing all ask for, may they all be granted - and may they all be mine and mine only!

And no one sings out aloud; there is a deafening silence.

Over my dead body!

Nasrudin and his friends are at the inn, drinking tea. *What,* says one of them, *would you like your family and friends to say when you are dead and they gather round your coffin?*

Each man at the table takes turn to muse over what he'd like to hear.

Oh, I'd like them to look at me, says one of the men, and to say: *Oh, we have lost our town's best teacher!*

Another man at the table says: *Oh, when I'm dead, I'd like them to say: Oh what a wonderful husband, a marvelous friend and loving father our town has lost!*

Yet another man says: I'd like them to say: *We've lost the town's cleverest man!*

But Nasrudin is quiet. So one of the men elbows Nasrudin and says: *Nasrudin, what would you like us to say at your funeral?*

And Nasrudin says: *Oh look - he's still moving!*

Nasrudin and the end of the world

There was a time when Nasrudin's town was filled with end-of-the-world zealots.

All they talked about was when the world would end, and who would go to heaven and who would go to hell when the world ended.

Many people declared themselves as leaders who had had divine inspiration as to when the world was ending and instructed their followers on what they should do to prepare themselves for this catastrophic event. Many quoted holy texts and holy books to pronounce when the world would end.

Nasrudin and his friends were drinking at the town inn. There was much talk about the end of the world and how it would end.

When is the end of the world, Nasrudin? asked one of the men at the table.

Ah, said Nasrudin, *when I die, that is the end of the world.*

How is that? asked another friend.

Well, it is the end of the world for me - and that's the long and short of it! replied Nasrudin.

Measurements of the world

The street before Nasrudin's home.

Nasrudin sits on the pavement and his donkey stands beside him. They are both looking at the townsfolk going about their lives.

1
A group of four men sees Nasrudin and his donkey. They walk up to him to make fun of him.
The moment the donkey sees the four men coming towards Nasrudin, the donkey brays: *Hee-haw!*

Ah Nasrudin, says one of the four men. *They say even your donkey's hee-haw has meaning! So what did the donkey just say?*
Oh, says Nasrudin, *it was wondering aloud what four donkeys are doing without their master.*
And the donkey brays again: *Hee-haw!*

2

But the group of men is not about to give up.
Tell us, says the strongest of the four men. *Tell us, O wise Nasrudin - tell us of the length and breadth and the depth of this our world, of this our earth.*

Just then a group of mourners passes by, carrying a coffin.

Follow him! says Nasrudin, pointing to the corpse in the coffin. *Follow him: he has measured the length and breadth and the depth of our world, of this our earth – and he is going there now. Quick, follow him and he will show you the answer!*

And the donkey brays: *Hee-haw! Hee-haw!*

Nasrudin: how do you know it's me?

1

A renowned philosopher on his travels set up tent outside Nasrudin's town and ridiculed the people of the town. He demanded the town pay him a thousand gold coins as reward for his brilliance, and so that he would spare them his insults.

His letter to the Town Council was full of derogatory phrases like: *you parochial and ignorant townsfolk...you unwashed and lice-infested fools whose only wise person is the most foolish in the world...a town incapable of providing any sensible answers...*

And in his letter he challenged the town to ask him any question that would stun him, even if but momentarily. If the town could do so, he would leave immediately and never bother the town again.

And the Mayor called Nasrudin and read out the letter to Nasrudin. The Mayor then blamed him for the town's shame and predicament for he had earned for himself the reputation of a fool and this was what had drawn the philosopher's attention to the town.

2

And so Nasrudin ran into the philosopher's tent and he
shouted to the philosopher:
Have you ever seen me before?

And the philosopher sneered and he shouted: *NO!*

And Nasrudin said: *But if you've never seen me before,
how do you know it's me?*

And the philosopher kept his word and packed up and
left immediately.

Nasrudin is very concerned

A group of Nasrudin's townsfolk came to see Nasrudin.

Nasrudin, they said. *We are a group of concerned citizens. We'd like you to join our group.*

Has the town council rewarded or recognized you yet for your concern? asked Nasrudin.
No, they said.
Have you been rewarded for your concern by anyone? asked Nasrudin.

We are concerned citizens but not concerned about rewards or recognition as we believe rewards corrupt human beings, said the leader of the group.

And Nasrudin said: *Oh, then I'm very concerned and cannot join your group - for if you are not interested in rewards and recognition, then you must be after something even more dangerous.*

Nasrudin: the generous dad

Nasrudin's son came running to Nasrudin and he said:
*Dad! What a generous dad you are! I dreamt last night
that you gave me 5 silver coins!*

Nasrudin looked at his son and he said: *Ah, since you
are a clever boy, I'll let you keep the 5 silver coins.
You'll never have to return it to me and you can spend it
any way you like!*

Nasrudin on the roof

Nasrudin was up on his roof, replacing some loose and cracked tiles.

Hey, Nasrudin; my dear friend! shouted a man standing in the street, just below Nasrudin's home.

It was a friend of Nasrudin from the other side of town. Nasrudin had not seen him in over six months. This man was a habitual borrower and always reluctant to return what he borrowed.

Yes, dear friend, shouted back Nasrudin.

Come down here, Nasrudin, shouted the friend. *I have something to say to you that ought not to be shouted out from down here.*

And so Nasrudin got off the roof and climbed down the ladder and stood before his friend.
Yes, you can tell me now what you want to say, said Nasrudin.

The friend smiled and he whispered: *Can I borrow twenty silver coins?*

Come with me up to the roof, said Nasrudin and he climbed up the ladder and sat down on his roof.

The friend followed and once the friend was seated beside him, Nasrudin said: *As your question could only be whispered standing below in the street, so my answer can only be whispered sitting on the roof. The answer is, my dear friend, NO.*

Nasrudin: small fish; big fish

Many renowned scholars and great personalities passing through Nasrudin's town stopped to meet Nasrudin.

Some wanted to see him because they thought he was wise; many wanted to see him in order to amuse themselves with what they thought was Nasrudin's stupidity, and thus relieve themselves of the boredom and artificiality of all their learning.

As for Nasrudin, the only thing that interested him in meeting all these people was that they always paid for his drinks and food at the best of the local inns.

One day, Great Scholar from the Imperial City was passing through the town where Nasrudin lived and he invited Nasrudin for lunch.

And so, Nasrudin sat down with Great Scholar at the Pumpkin, the town's most expensive restaurant and which served the best fish in the region.

Nasrudin provided polite and short answers to Great Scholar's questions and when the waiter brought in two plates of cooked fish, Nasrudin immediately took the plate with the bigger fish.

That's outrageous! said Great Scholar, looking rather angry. *Nasrudin – you shouldn't have done that! You should be ashamed of yourself, Nasrudin!*

And Nasrudin said: *Why, Great Scholar of the Imperial City?*

Because, said Great Scholar, *in taking the bigger fish for yourself, you have been selfish - and have thus acted contrary to the sacred principles of every known civilized tradition and all morality and theology, and in contradiction to all acceptable principles! Shame on you, Nasrudin!*

Nasrudin placed his fingers nervously on the edge of his plate, and he said to Great Scholar: *Why, Sir, what would you have done?*

And the Great Scholar said: *Well, I would not have done such a shameless thing. I would have offered the plate with the bigger fish to the other person and I would have taken the plate with the smaller fish. That is the honorable thing to do.*

Ah, Sir! said Nasrudin. *Then I have saved you the trouble! You do have the smaller fish and so eat with honor, gratitude - and eat it proudly!*

And Nasrudin ate his bigger fish with much relish and delight.

Nasrudin's contrary ride

Ah, Nasrudin was always coming up with new tricks to amuse the people and the children around him…perhaps in amusing them Nasrudin also taught people something about life…

There were many things he did but one of the strangest things he did was to ride his donkey though the streets - sitting with his back to the donkey's head!

Yes – he rode his donkey with his donkey facing one way and he himself seated so that he had his back to the donkey's head!

Why did he do that?

No one knows. People pressed him to tell them why he rode his donkey with his back to the donkey's head, and he would laugh – and he would offer a reason that was different to the one he had just given...Ah, Nasrudin…one may never know why he did it, but he certainly brought laughter and mirth into the hearts of the people of the town…

Strange sight

Look at this strange sight! laugh the children and the people.
Nasrudin rides his donkey but he sits with his back to the donkey's head! Ha! Ha! Nasrudin rides facing one way and his donkey the other! Come and see! Ha! Ha!

Nasrudin: turn around

Look at this strange sight! laugh the children and the people.
Nasrudin rides his donkey but he sits with his back to the donkey's head! Ha! Ha! Nasrudin rides facing one way and his donkey the other! Come and see! Ha! Ha!

Hey, Nasrudin! Why do you ride your donkey facing one way and you the other?

Well my dear friend, says Nasrudin, *I just changed my mind about the direction in which I am to travel, and I am waiting for my donkey to turn around.*

Nasrudin: in anger

Hey, Nasrudin! Why do you ride your donkey facing one way and the donkey the other?

Well, my dear friend, says Nasrudin, *my donkey and I are no longer on speaking terms!*

Nasrudin: shame

Hey, Nasrudin! Why do you ride your donkey with your back to your donkey's head?

Ah, my dear friend, says Nasrudin. *My greedy donkey ate its week's supply of food within an hour - and I'm parading the donkey through the streets in this ridiculous manner in order to shame the donkey!*

Nasrudin: opposing will

Hey, Nasrudin! Why is your donkey facing one way and you the opposite direction?

That's a question, my dear friend, says Nasrudin, *you should ask my stubborn donkey. You should ask my donkey: Why don't you go in the direction your master wants to go?*

Nasrudin: wrongs and rights

Nasrudin and his friends sat round a table at the tea-house.

They sat drinking tea with a learned visitor.

The world, said the visitor, *will be a better place only when one thing happens.*

And what is that? asked one of Nasrudin's friends at the table.

Ah, said the visitor, looking very wise and important, *when each feels as strongly indignant as the one who has been wronged, then the world will be a better place.*

Everyone at the table nodded approvingly and admiringly, except Nasrudin.

What do you think, Nasrudin? said the visitor.

And Nasrudin said:
One is not wronged until one can find no blessing in an event.

Nasrudin: tapioca flour and garlic

1

Nasrudin! shouts Nasrudin's wife. *Nasrudin, go to the town-center immediately and get me a bag of tapioca flour and ten cloves of garlic.*

Nasrudin jumps up from his chair. *I'll do that!* he says gladly, and he walks out to the shed where his donkey is.
Donkey, says Nasrudin.
Hee-haw! replies donkey.
Let's go to the town-center and get a bag of tapioca flour and ten cloves of garlic.
Hee-haw! says donkey.

Ah, see how gladly Nasrudin and his donkey make their way to the town-center – the donkey glad to be out of its shed, and Nasrudin glad to be out of his house.

2

And as Nasrudin rides his donkey, Nasrudin sings to
himself:
A bag of tapioca flour
and ten cloves of garlic.

He does this so he will not forget what his wife told him
to buy:
A bag of tapioca flour
and ten cloves of garlic.

3

Nasrudin and his donkey pass Fifth Street. A woman has
set up store along the pavement and she is selling some
mutton soup. The aroma of the mutton soup dances in
the air.

Nasrudin says: *Ah, donkey - what a wonderful aroma*
that mutton soup has...That aroma of the mutton soup
fills all my senses, donkey...

But Nasrudin will not stop; he will not be distracted. He
has a purpose. So he and donkey continue determined
towards the town-center; and Nasrudin continues to sing
so that he will remember what he is to buy at the town-
center.

Ah, see how gleefully Nasrudin and his donkey make
their way to the town-center, and Nasrudin is singing all
the time:
Mutton soup
and ten cloves of garlic.

And donkey joins Nasrudin:
Hee-haw!
Hee-haw!

4

Nasrudin and his donkey now pass Portal Street.
And Nasrudin is singing:
Mutton soup
and ten cloves of garlic.

A woman has set up store along the pavement and she is
selling some strawberry pies. The aroma of the
strawberry pies dances in the air.
Nasrudin says: *Ah, donkey, what a wonderful aroma*
those strawberry pies have…That aroma of the
strawberry pies fills all my senses, donkey…

But Nasrudin will not stop; he will not be distracted. He
has a purpose. So he and donkey continue determined
towards the town-center; and Nasrudin continues to sing
so that he will remember what he is to buy at the town-
center.

Ah, see how gleefully Nasrudin and his donkey make
their way to the center, and Nasrudin is singing all the
time:
*Strawberry pies
and mutton soup.*

And donkey joins Nasrudin:
*Hee-haw!
Hee-haw!*

And throughout the streets as he nears the town-center,
Nasrudin sings aloud:
*Strawberry pies
and mutton soup.*

And always his faithful donkey repeats what he says:
*Hee-haw!
Hee-haw!*

5

Nasrudin and his donkey arrive at the town-centre.
Nasrudin remembers clearly what his wife asked him to
buy, and even now he sings to himself:
Strawberry pies
and mutton soup.

And everyone enjoys listening to Nasrudin's song; they
just love his music and the donkey's music too.
Strawberry pies
and mutton soup.

Hee-haw!
Hee-haw!

And so Nasrudin buys an earthen pot of mutton soup and
a dozen strawberry pies wrapped in banana leaves.

There are many distractions and attractions at the town-
center but Nasrudin will not linger long. He will not be
distracted. He has a purpose. So he and donkey set out
on their return journey - determined towards home.

And Nasrudin, happy that he has remembered what his
wife had asked him to buy, sings all the way home:
Strawberry pies
and mutton soup.

6

And as he passes Portal Street, Nasrudin smells the
aroma of the strawberry pies, and Nasrudin says:
*Ah donkey, how silly of me. I could have bought the
strawberry pies here instead of going all the way to the
city-center!*

And Nasrudin continues on his journey home.

Ah, see how gleefully Nasrudin and his donkey make
their way home and Nasrudin is singing all the time:
*Strawberry pies
and mutton soup.*

And all along the way, donkey joins Nasrudin:
*Hee-haw!
Hee-haw!*

It is such sweet music.

7

And as he passes Fifth Street, Nasrudin smells the
aroma of the mutton soup, and Nasrudin says:
*Ah donkey, how silly of me. I could have bought the
mutton soup here instead of going all the way to the city-
center!*

And Nasrudin continues on his journey home.

Ah, see how gleefully Nasrudin and his donkey make
their way home and Nasrudin is singing all the time:
*Strawberry pies
and mutton soup.*

And donkey joins Nasrudin:
*Hee-haw!
Hee-haw!*

It is such sweet music.

8

And when they reach home, donkey goes to its shed and
Nasrudin goes inside his house.

And all the while Nasrudin goes in singing:
*Strawberry pies
and mutton soup –*
and when Nasrudin's wife sees the mutton soup
and strawberry pies Nasrudin has bought, poor
Nasrudin! – *he now faces a different kind of music*!

And listening to the shrill but heavenly music coming from Nasrudin's home, the donkey in its shed sings along:

Hee-haw!
Hee-haw!
Hee-haw!
Hee-haw!

Nasrudin, can I borrow donkey?

A friend of Nasrudin from the other side of town comes to visit Nasrudin.
Nasrudin and the friend sit at Nasrudin's dining table with a view to the garden.

Ah, says Nasrudin's friend. *What a nice table you have.*

Nasrudin places his hands on his table and he says:
Yes...thank you...

Ah, says Nasrudin's friend. *What a nice view you have to your garden.*
Nasrudin looks towards his window and he says:
Yes...thank you...

Nasrudin, I'll come to the purpose of my visit, says Nasrudin's friend.

Nasrudin nods nervously and he says: *Yes, thank you.*

Nasrudin, says his friend. *I have to transport some goods to the next town. Please lend me your donkey.*

Sorry, says Nasrudin swiftly. *I've already lent my donkey to a neighbor.*

Just then there is a loud braying from the garden: *Hee-haw! Hee-haw!*

What's that? shouts the neighbor, jumping up from his seat.

That's a hee-haw! says Nasrudin, nervously.

You lied, Nasrudin! shouts the neighbor, outraged. *That's your donkey in the garden! You lied that you lent it to your neighbor but I just heard your donkey in the garden!*

My dear friend, says Nasrudin. *My dear friend – whom would you rather believe? Would you rather believe me or would you rather believe a donkey?*

donkey philosophy

someone says:
this is life;
and many have each a say;
Nasrudin's donkey is quiet
but one says:
you are wrong; I'll tell you what life is –
and makes a grand pronouncement...
Nasrudin's donkey laughs and spits in the air

someone says
this is love;
and many have each a say;
Nasrudin's donkey is quiet
but one says:
you are wrong; I'll tell you what love is –
and makes a grand pronouncement…

Nasrudin's donkey laughs and rolls in the dust with
laughter
and *ooops*! - donkey makes a rude noise in the posterior
and the cosmic dust flies
and covers all of earth

Nasrudin: who are you?

1

Nasrudin, are you - asked a visitor – *are you a fool, or are you a wise fool? Are you a wise man pretending to be a fool or a fool mistaken for a wise man? Are you a simpleton whose words and actions are taken beyond their context and wisdom ascribed to foolishness? Are you a pretender who exploits the art of the silly and the vague? Are you an innocent blessed by the Almighty?*

Nasrudin smiled, and he said: *I'm Nasrudin, and that animal you see outside the inn and scratching its nose against the window, that animal is my donkey.*

2

And the visitor smiled. And he said: *And what is Nasrudin?*

And Nasrudin smiled, and he said:

I have whirled and twirled
east, west and north and south
and I have turned and danced
and I have delved within too –
and nowhere is found
what one may describe as Nasrudin
or any other.

Nasrudin, the egg and dust

1

Nasrudin was sitting on a chair along the road and eating a boiled egg.
The donkey stood in the shade of a tree nearby, kicking up dust.

2

One of Nasrudin's friends noticed this and he shouted to Nasrudin:
Why are sitting on a chair along the road and eating an egg?

And Nasrudin replied:
Why, would you have me eat the chair and sit on the egg?

Hee-haw! Hee-haw! brayed the donkey.

3

And why, said the friend, *is your donkey kicking up dust below that tree?*

Why, would you have the donkey kick me instead? said Nasrudin.

Hee-haw! Hee-haw! brayed the donkey.

Nasrudin's friend shook his head at Nasrudin and his donkey and walked away.

Nasrudin: who's the boss?

Nasrudin and his friends were sitting in the tavern, drinking.
The sun was setting and the inn-keeper lit a thick, tall candle.

Nasrudin's friends talked and sang happily.
Nasrudin, however, kept looking nervously at the candle.
His friends grew louder and louder.

OK, said Nasrudin suddenly, as the candle had burned off a quarter of itself. *I've got to go. My wife said that when the first tavern candle is burned to its first quarter, I must be on my way home. So I'd better go.*

Nasrudin! shouted one of Nasrudin's friends at the table. *You'd better teach your wife who's the boss in your home!*

Oh - said Nasrudin – *she already knows!*

And Nasrudin left as quickly as he could.

Nasrudin's speeches

1

Nasrudin was asked to give a speech at the city hall.

Nasrudin arrived at the hall, looked at the eager crowd and he said:
Do you, gentle people of my beloved town – do you know what I am about to say?

NO! came the unanimous reply.

Nasrudin shook his head. *I have no wish*, he said to his audience, *to speak to ignorant people who have no idea of what I am about to say.*

And Nasrudin walked out of the hall, jumped up on his donkey's back and rode away.

But the Mayor quickly came running after him and invited him to return to the hall, and to speak to the audience.

2

And so Nasrudin returned to the hall, looked at the eager
crowd and he said:
Do you, gentle people of my beloved town – do you know
what I am about to say?

YES! came the unanimous reply.

Nasrudin shook his head. *There is no need then*, he said
to his audience, *to speak to people who know what I am*
about to say.

And Nasrudin walked out of the hall, jumped up on his
donkey's back and rode away.
But the Mayor again quickly came running after
Nasrudin and invited him to return to the hall, and to
speak to the audience.

3

Nasrudin arrived at the hall a third time, looked at the
eager crowd, and he said:
Do you, gentle people of my beloved town – do you know
what I am about to say?

NO! came the spontaneous reply from half the crowd.
YES! came the loud reply, just as spontaneous, from the
other half of the crowd.

Nasrudin shook his head. And Nasrudin said: *Those who*
do not know what I was about to say should remain
quiet; and those who know what I was about to say

should tell those who don't know what I was about to say!

And Nasrudin walked out of the hall, jumped up on his donkey's back and rode away.

4

And the donkey grumbled: *Hee-haw! Hee-haw! Hee-haw!*

And Nasrudin said: *No, donkey. The Mayor won't call us again. In fact, I've got a feeling we won't have to go there ever again! Let us now ride to the northern hill; and let us rest there for the rest of the day in the cool shade of our favorite tree.*

And the donkey brayed: *Hee-haw!*

Nasrudin and the Great Visitor

1

One day, Nasrudin was lying down in the shade of a tree on the northern hill.

The town mayor sent a messenger to Nasrudin.

You are to proceed immediately, said the messenger, *to the city hall where a Great Visitor and teacher from the capital city is here to speak on his great teachings.*

Nasrudin had no choice but to obey and so he got up and rode on his donkey to the city hall.

There were hundreds of braying donkeys tied to posts outside the city hall, and Nasrudin tied his donkey to the last post available.

Stay here, donkey, said Nasrudin. *I'll be back. And don't keep braying like the other donkeys!*

Hee-haw! Hee-haw! brayed the cheeky donkey.

2

The town hall was packed with people and Nasrudin sat
amongst the crowd on the floor.
The mayor introduced the visiting speaker: *...there is no
one who has not heard of our most distinguished
visitor...he is world-renowned and holds many titles and
is first in the Emperor's Order of Speakers...*

There was tremendous applause and the Great Visitor
made a lengthy speech. The speech went on and on...the
Great Visitor spoke about truth; about the great
fundamentals of truth, and of the allusions to truth in the
world's great traditions and...the speaker made very
many learned inter-textual and inter-disciplinary
references from since ancient times and...
And the speech just went on and on...

Suddenly the Great Speaker fell silent and pointed a
finger at Nasrudin.
You! shouted the Great Visitor, still pointing his finger at
Nasrudin. *Are you sleeping during my Grand Talk?*

No, Sir! said Nasrudin. *I am, during your Grand Talk,
trying very hard to stay awake!*

Nasrudin and the wild tigers

Bong! Bong! Dong! Bong-Dong!
That noise is coming out of Nasrudin's home.
And *Hee-haw! Hee-haw!*
That noise is coming out of donkey's shed.

This racket goes on the whole morning.
The noise wakes up everyone in the neighborhood and
everyone's got a splitting headache!
And it does not seem the noise will end.

Bong! Bong! Dong! Bong-Dong!
That noise is coming out of Nasrudin's home.
And *Hee-haw! Hee-haw!*
That noise is coming out of donkey's shed.
The noise continues even into the evening.

The neighbors gather outside Nasrudin's home and they
shout out to Nasrudin.

Hey, Nasrudin! Stop the noise and come out! shouts one.
Hey Nasrudin! shouts another.

Nasrudin and the donkey come running out happily to
meet the crowd.

Yes, my good neighbors. What are you here for?
Nasrudin says.
The donkey remains silent, preferring to allow the
master to do the talking.

Nasrudin! shouts one of the men in the crowd. *What's
all this noise from your house and your donkey's shed?*

Oh, my dear friends, says Nasrudin, *I was playing on the
drums and my donkey was braying aloud. You see, my
friends - my donkey and I are trying to keep away wild
tigers from entering our town!*
Hee-haw! Hee-haw! agrees the donkey.

But Nasrudin, says one of the women, *there are no
tigers for thousands of miles round our town!*

And Nasrudin pats his donkey on its back, and he
declares: *Good! You see, our effort is working! Indeed,
we've exceeded our own expectations.!*

And the donkey says: *Hee-haw! Hee-haw!*

Nasrudin: sun and moon

Nasrudin was riding on his donkey through the streets
when a child waved at him to stop.
Yes, dear child? said Nasrudin. *What is it you want?*

Sir, said the child. My teacher asked my class a question
and maybe you can help me answer the question. I have
to bring a good answer to class tomorrow.

Well, ask me, dear child, said Nasrudin.

Sir, said the child. *Which is more important? The sun or
the moon?*

Ha! What an easy question! said Nasrudin.
And Nasrudin's donkey laughed.
That's an easy question, Nasrudin repeated. *Of course
the moon is more important than the sun!*

Why is that, sir? asked the child.

*Because the sun shines when it's already day; the moon,
however,* said Nasrudin, *shines when it's dark and that
is when we really need the light!*

And the donkey laughed: *Hee-haw! Hee-haw!*

Nasrudin and the barbarians

1

It was morning and Nasrudin rode on his donkey to one of the western hills.
Beyond the western hills were isolated villages, whose people Nasrudin's townsfolk despised and called barbarians.

The western hills were far away from the town center.
The hills were always quiet except for the melody of singing birds and the warbling streams, and
Nasrudin enjoyed many hours of quiet and solitude there.
The donkey too loved coming here. It would sleep for the most part of the sojourn and when inclined to do so, prance around the trees and bushes, chasing butterflies.

And so Nasrudin lay down in the shade of a tree on a hill. He listened to the birds, admired the colors of the trees round him, and soon fell asleep.

2

Nasrudin woke up suddenly. He had heard a loud noise. The donkey was still sleeping in the shade of a tree a few meters away.

Then Nasrudin saw a villager cutting a tree nearby.

Nasrudin was quite angry with the villager for having woken him.

You barbarian! shouted Nasrudin.

The villager dropped his axe on to the ground, and obviously afraid, he came to Nasrudin and he said in a low voice: *Sir. I am sorry for waking you up. I did not know you and your donkey were here. I am sorry for disrupting your civilized activity.*

Oh, you barbarian! repeated Nasrudin.

Please sir, said the villager. *Many from your town have called me barbarian. Could you teach me to be civilized?*

And Nasrudin glared at the villager and he said: *It's simple. I'll give you an instant guide. Pick on anyone who is physically and socially weaker than you are and call that person a barbarian! Do this at least three times a month to different people and do it so others can hear you! Very soon, you will be considered civilized.*

And the villager thanked Nasrudin and he left immediately for his village, for truly he could not wait to practice the art of being civilized.

Nasrudin and the moon

1

It was night and Nasrudin was thirsty.
He went to the well in his compound.
He grabbed a bucket, tied a rope to the bucket and
walked to the well.

Nasrudin looked down into the well.

There, down in the well, he saw the moon reflected in
the water.
Oh no! he screamed. *The moon's fallen into the well!*

The donkey heard Nasrudin's scream and came running
out of its shed.
The donkey looked into the well.

Look, donkey! shouted Nasrudin. *The moon's fallen into
the well!*

Hee-haw! Hee-haw! wailed the donkey.

I'll save it! Nasrudin said. *Do not worry! I'll save the
moon!*

2

Nasrudin placed the bucket upside down on the ground
beside the well. He stood on the bucket, leaned over the
well, and he used a long stick to reach to the moon down
in the well. And Nasrudin tried to flick the moon up
back to the sky. He did this a few times.
Then suddenly he slipped, the bucket rolled over, and he
fell just beside it.
He fell with his back on the ground.
Nasrudin could see the sky. And the moon! Nasrudin
saw that the moon was in the sky!

I've saved the moon! he shouted. *With the stick, I've
flicked the moon back to the sky!*

Nasrudin's donkey ran round the well and brayed
happily: *Hee-haw! Hee-haw!*

I've saved the moon! shouted Nasrudin again. Lying
there on the ground, he raised his hands towards the sky
and he sang aloud: *I flicked the moon back to the sky! I
saved the moon!*

Nasrudin: I have needs too

1

Nasrudin and his friend were sitting and talking in the shade below a tree on the northern hill.
Nasrudin's donkey lay in the shade, just a few meters away.

Just then two strangers approached Nasrudin and his friend.
Please Sirs, said one of the strangers. *We are homeless. Could you share some of your food as we are very hungry?*

Nasrudin's donkey got up on its feet immediately on hearing these words.

2

Nasrudin's friend said: *Of course I will. I will give you my full packet of food I brought with me.*
And Nasrudin's friend immediately gave his packet of food to one of the strangers.

Nasrudin looked at his donkey and then at the second stranger, and he said: *I will give you one-third of the food in my packet* – and so Nasrudin did.

The two strangers ate and left after thanking Nasrudin
and his friend for their kindness.

3

Then Nasrudin's friend said to him: *Nasrudin – that was
mean of you. They looked extremely hungry. You should
have given them your whole packet, as I did.*

And Nasrudin replied:
*Oh, I gave him only one-third as my donkey and I too
have our needs!*
And Nasrudin called out to his donkey and he said:
*Come, donkey. Let us eat. My friend here does not
hunger until evening today when he returns home.*

And Nasrudin's donkey came running to him, braying
gleefully: *Hee-haw! Hee-haw!*

Nasrudin hurt and bruised

Nasrudin appeared at the town tavern, bruised and his right arm bandaged.
What happened to you? asked a friend, as Nasrudin sat down at a table.

Oh, nothing much, said Nasrudin. Last evening, my wife threw a black shirt down the stairs.

But how did you get hurt, Nasrudin? asked the friend, puzzled.

Oh, quite by chance; I happened to be wearing that black shirt! said Nasrudin.

Nasrudin and the wild bear

1

Nasrudin went to the annual local fair.
The fair was getting bigger and more showy each year.
This year a wild bear the size of five strong men was the center of attraction.

2

The bear was kept in a huge cage.
A dignitary from a nearby city said that his wife wanted to see the bear dance.
So the dignitary's followers brought it out of the cage and tied the bear to a tree. Then they poked it with stakes and with their knives.
They beat the bear and struck its feet with large poles.

3

The dignitary and his wife stood by laughing as they watched the bear dancing in pain.
A crowd gathered round the tree and the bear, and everyone clapped.
Nasrudin sat at a tea-stall, drinking tea and observing people. This was always his favorite activity wherever he went.

4

Suddenly the bear broke free and it ran about wildly.
The dignitary fell on the ground and his wife fell into a
pool of muddy water.
The crowd ran to protect the dignitary while the
dignitary's followers went to rescue the lady.
When Nasrudin saw what was happening, he
immediately jumped on his donkey and rode home
swiftly and locked himself up in his house!

5

Two days later the Mayor saw Nasrudin at the local inn.
The Mayor admonished Nasrudin.
Nasrudin! the mayor yelled. *Everyone at the fair was
trying to help the visiting dignitary and his wife but you
just ran away!*
I didn't run away, said Nasrudin. *I got out of everyone's
way!*

Rubbish! said the Mayor. *It was foolish of you to do such
a thing! You should have stayed and you should have
helped the visiting dignitary and his wife. You should
have protected the reputation of our town by staying and
protecting the visiting dignitary and his wife! It was
truly foolish of you, Nasrudin!*

Not more foolish, Sir, said Nasrudin, *than letting the
wild animal out of its cage!*

Why is Nasrudin's donkey happy?

Nasrudin, asked a neighbor. *Why are you always happy?*

Because I am moderate in all things; I do not go too far, or go too little.

And how is it your donkey is always happy?

I know its strength and do not overburden it, said Nasrudin. *So, my dear neighbor, whether it's the donkey or me, it's the same principle: moderation.*

Nasrudin: heaven, hell and going nowhere

Nasrudin was seated in the shade of a tree on the hill-top and the donkey rested nearby.
A man came running up to Nasrudin.

Sitting down on the grass before Nasrudin, the man said: *I'm afraid. I'm truly afraid.*

Why are you afraid? asked Nasrudin.

And the man said: *A group of men in black and grey talked to me and they declared I was going to hell.*

And Nasrudin said:
Well, those who believe in Hell will go to Hell; those who believe in Heaven will go to Heaven. So choose your belief well.
But those who neither believe in Hell or Heaven don't go anywhere. They are where they are; for such people, there is no going or coming; they are just where they are without fear, without expectation, without anxiety.

And the man looked at Nasrudin's donkey which lay on the ground, happily chewing grass, and he asked: *And what about your donkey? Will it go to Heaven or will it go to Hell?*

And Nasrudin said:
Mostly it goes where I tell it to go; but sometimes in its stubborn moments, I go where it goes.

Nasrudin sees a violent man

Nasrudin and his donkey were out one Spring morning, enjoying the day.

Suddenly, Nasrudin and his donkey heard a loud cry.

The donkey turned round, and Nasrudin and the donkey saw a man at the edge of the town river. The man was furiously beating his wife with a rusty metal pipe, and the woman was screaming out in pain.

Then the man threw the metal pipe far out into the river. And he turned to the woman and he shouted: *I am your husband! I can do anything I want! That is the law!*

Nasrudin quickly jumped off his donkey, ran and jumped into the river, and touched the spot where the metal pipe had fallen, and swiftly returned to the shore.

The man saw this and he asked Nasrudin: *What did you just do?*

Nasrudin sat himself on his donkey and he said: *Oh, I marked the spot where your metal pipe fell, so you can easily find it - just in case you want to use it again.*

And the donkey said: *Hee-haw*! and trotted away slowly, carrying its master.

Nasrudin's cheeky days

Though in later years Nasrudin was poor, he came from a wealthy family.
Nasrudin's father was a rich merchant and owned many slave girls.

One night, when Nasrudin was still a young man, he crept into the bed of one of his father's favorite slave girls.

The slave girl, startled, said: *Nasrudin. What do you want? Why are you here?*

And Nasrudin said:
Am I Nasrudin? Are you blind! Can't you see I'm my father?

Nasrudin's tall tale

Nasrudin was with the local drunks in the town inn.
Each drunk told a tall tale of the most improbable events
and impossible happenings.

Everyone now turned to Nasrudin. *Tell us an
extraordinary thing about yourself!* shouted a drunk.

Nasrudin smiled and he said: *What is most amazing is
that I am still just as strong as I was when I was young.*

All the drunks laughed. Only *drunks and fools will
believe that kind of nonsense! We are neither drunks nor
fools!* they said.

Well, Nasrudin said. *You all know that huge rock outside
our town inn. You see, I couldn't carry that huge rock
when I was young - and you know what? - I still can't
carry it in my old age! So I'm still as strong just as when
I was young!*

Nasrudin's prayer

Nasrudin was, like most people, often short of money.

One day, Nasrudin and his donkey were both hungry but Nasrudin had no money.
Even as he was seated on his donkey, riding through the streets of his town, Nasrudin prayed aloud:
Oh, Almighty Lord! Let me find a silver coin now on the ground and I will praise your name every minute of my life!

And the donkey agreed and said earnestly: *Hee-haw! Hee-haw*!

And then suddenly, a few minutes later, the donkey stopped and brayed excitedly:
Hee-haw! Hee-haw!
The donkey was pointing to something on the ground.
Nasrudin jumped off the donkey and on to the ground, and he picked up a gold coin.

And Nasrudin turned to his donkey and he said: *Ah, we will not go hungry for a week!*
And the donkey laughed happily: *Hee-haw! Hee-haw!*

And Nasrudin looked up towards the sky and he said:
*Dear Almighty Lord – don't bother about sending me
that silver coin. My donkey and I've already found a
coin. In fact my donkey and I did better than a silver
coin – we found a gold coin! So, really, don't worry
about it, Almighty Lord!*

And the donkey agreed: *Hee-haw! Hee-haw!*

Nasrudin, donkey, the Professor and Identity

1

A professor and eminent philosopher from the Seur
University, of the ancient City of Suri, was on his
travels. He stopped at Nasrudin's town to rest, and
hearing that Nasrudin was the wisest man in this
insignificant town, he invited Nasrudin to visit him at
Dignity Room in the town tavern.

But the answer came from Nasrudin promptly:
*Sir, it may inconvenience all concerned, especially my
donkey - for the donkey may find it difficult staying
unperturbed in an enclosed and stuffy space as the
Dignity Room. Let us meet therefore in the shade of the
tree on top of the northern hill.*

Amused, the Professor went to the tree on top of the northern hill, where he found Nasrudin and the donkey waiting for him.

Nasrudin and the Professor sat down in the shade below the tree; and the donkey stood within a respectable but within hearing distance.

2

Nasrudin, said the Professor, *let me first introduce myself.*
I am the Professor Eminence, Foremost, and of the Order of the Bulei by Imperial Appointment. I have various chairs of Antiquity of Kring and Various Appointments overseeing the education of the Imperial Territory. The University I teach at is of the Royal City of Suri, beyond compare in the annals of human achievement and since the beginning of recorded history.
I preside over research into Identity and Human Meaning and also oversee all philosophical deliberations and cogitations on human thought. Seur, Nasrudin, is the center of learning; there is no learning without Seur.

The professor stopped and looked at Nasrudin.
Nasrudin looked dazed.
Hee-haw! Hee-haw! the donkey laughed.

The Professor was quite annoyed and he asked
Nasrudin: *Why does your donkey laugh?*

And Nasrudin said:
*Oh, it says it marvels at your lengthy exposition of who
you are and what you are, and how you even ascribe a
precise and concrete identity for your specialization. In
this context, donkey wonders what there will be if there
were no identity.*

The Professor experienced a stillness in his mind he had
never experienced before.

Nasrudin and the dying man

The old man was dying.
One by one his relatives visited him. Even relatives and
friends he had not seen for years called on him to say
farewell. They all expressed their deep love for him.
And as each came to him, the old man held each
person's hands and spoke to each.

To one he said: *Yes, I love you.*
To another he said: *I go without any ill-will.*
To yet another he said: *Peace be with you.*

And so to each person he said such nice and kind words.

And then the old man called for Nasrudin.
And when Nasrudin came in, he stood one side and observed everyone, and listened to what they said and what the dying man said to them.

And then Nasrudin raised his hands in the air, and when everyone was turned to hear him, Nasrudin said: *Fools! Why did you not visit him in his good health? You loved him not when healthy and living, but you love him dying!*

And Nasrudin turned to the dying man and he shouted: *Fool! Why did you not live with such nice feelings all the days when you were energetic and fully alive?*

And Nasrudin then left the scene.

And the old man smiled and he said: *At last I have heard the truth. It is a blessing to die having heard the truth.*

And the old man died peacefully.

And the others? They returned to their normal business of life and continued as they always had been.

And Nasrudin? When he returned to his donkey just outside the dying man's house, the donkey neighed: *Hee-haw! Hee-haw!*

And Nasrudin said: *Yes, I know...you're right...Live well; die well...*

Nasrudin: pure and holy

A group of travelers was passing through Nasrudin's
town and they requested to see Nasrudin.
And so Nasrudin sat with them below a tree, his donkey
tied to a branch of the tree.

Hee-haw! neighed the donkey.
Ah, my donkey says we can start, said Nasrudin.

The visitors laughed and the conversation turned to this
and that, and they started talking about purity and
holiness.

*I wash myself nine times a day in accordance with laws
given to the first Man,* declared a visitor from the East.
And therefore am I the holiest and the purest.

And a visitor from the North said:
*Ah, it is known that I am of the group that is purest of
the purest, the holiest of the holiest. All our scriptures
declare that and since I am one of that group, I am the
purest and I am the holiest.*

Another said:
I only eat pure vegetarian food. Therefore am I the purest and the holiest.

Ah, protested another, *I eat only food that is sanctified with holy prayer and therefore am I the holiest and the purest.*

And a visitor from the South said:
It is beyond dispute that my religion is the only True Religion for God has declared it so – and since my religion is the only True Religion, it follows that I am the purest and I am the holiest.

And a visitor from the West said:
Fools! It is decreed in the holiest scriptures that all posteriors should be washed with water from a well, and should be so washed thrice and vigorously so that no impurity remains – and as I have washed my posterior in no other way since my birth, there is none purer and holier than I.

And so each visitor put forward their claim as to their purity and their holiness.
Nasrudin's donkey bit leaves off the branch and spit the bitter bits onto the ground.

And Nasrudin remained silent.

But Nasrudin, said one of the visitors. *You are silent. Speak: Who is the holiest and the purest?*

And Nasrudin said: *Naturally I am the holiest and the purest – for I never speak of holiness or purity.*

And the donkey said: *Hee-haw! Hee-haw!*

And Nasrudin said to the visitors:
My donkey points to the irony of my last sentence and says I have just lost all my holiness and purity.

And the visitors remained silent, confounded by a donkey.

Nasrudin works a miracle

The townsfolk want a miracle

There was a group of very eloquent visitors to
Nasrudin's quiet town.
They impressed the simple people with their talk and
claims to be able to work miracles.

Many of the townsfolk spoke with Nasrudin about this.
And so they said to Nasrudin:
*See, these new people can work miracles. They say if we
have faith, they can work miracles.*

And Nasrudin said:
*True miracles are before you everyday. Each birth in
your homes, each tree and living thing...and love...all
these are miracles. All other miracles are just tricks any
magician can do.*

But the people would not listen and they said:
No! We want miracles! Nasrudin, we want miracles!

And Nasrudin said to his townsfolk:
*I too can work miracles but I have not boasted about it.
But I'll show you. Now, as you know, our town's
drought has lasted for over a year, with hardly any rain.
Gather all the people and come to the town hill and I
will perform a miracle. I will make it rain. Come with
faith and there will be a miracle!*

Miracle at the hilltop

And so the next day two hundred people gathered at the hilltop.
We are here to witness Nasrudin work a miracle! the people said to one another.

And Nasrudin came riding his donkey. He rode to the hilltop and he addressed the crowd.

Are you come for the miracle, my good people? Nasrudin asked.

Yes, Nasrudin! Make it rain! Our gardens need water! shouted the people.

I will work a miracle. Sure. But are you sure you come with faith, my good people? asked Nasrudin.

YES – WE COME WITH FAITH! came the spontaneous roar from the crowd. *GIVE US A MIRACLE! GIVE US RAIN NOW!*

You lie! - you faithless! shouted Nasrudin. *You say you come with faith – but if you have faith that I can make rain, where are your umbrellas? Not one of you has an umbrella! Go, you faithless! No miracles for those without faith!*

And the townsfolk walked away full of shame and regret for not having displayed their faith.

Nasrudin's contradictions

Nasrudin took a visitor round his town. Sometimes they rode through the town and sometimes they walked.

A young man stopped to talk to Nasrudin.
Nasrudin listened carefully to what the young man had to say and advised him accordingly, and ended the conversation by saying: *Young man, life can be difficult.*

Later an old woman stopped to talk to Nasrudin. Nasrudin listened carefully to what the old woman had to say and advised her accordingly, and ended the conversation by saying: *Respected lady, life is beautiful. Just find its beauty.*

When the woman had left, the visitor who had listened to the conversations, exclaimed:
Nasrudin! How can you say such contradictory things? To one person you say: Life is difficult; and to the other person you say life is beautiful! You do not know what you say!

And Nasrudin said:
Ah, dear friend...Do you blame a doctor for giving different medicine to different patients?

Nasrudin at life's tavern

1
Nasrudin was in the tavern with his friends and only
stumbled out of it at about 3am.
He sat on his donkey and let it take him where it would
in the dark.
Suddenly a night guard held the donkey by the rope
round its neck and he shouted at Nasrudin.
Sir, screamed the guard. *What are you doing here so late
in the dark?*

If I knew that, said Nasrudin, *I wouldn't be here, would
I?*

2

And then it was about 9am. The donkey had carried
Nasrudin through the same streets about seven times.
Nasrudin was tired and was lying flat on the donkey's
back, and holding on to the donkey's neck.
Nasrudin, said the local messenger. *I have a letter for
you.*

I am not Nasrudin, said Nasrudin.

You are most certainly Nasrudin, said the messenger. *I
have a letter for you.*

I do not think I am Nasrudin, said Nasrudin.

You most certainly are, insisted the messenger. *I deliver
letters and I know everyone in this town! You are
Nasrudin and that is who you are!*

And Nasrudin said:
*My dear man, you seem so certain as to who I am. All
my life I have tried to understand who I am and have
failed – and yet you insist I am Nasrudin. You seem to
know me better than I know myself! And though I have
yet to meet any who know themselves, you are one who
knows everyone! From this day, sir, my donkey and I
will follow you – for you are the wisest man to have
lived – for you know others who do not even know
themselves! Come, lead the way and we will follow!*

Nasrudin's flies

Nasrudin and his friend and his donkey sit in the shade of a tree.
The friends talk, the donkey brays, and they are all thirsty.

Nasrudin takes out a leather flask of water and a set of cups and a bowl.

He pours water in two cups and some water in a bowl.
The flies are all around them now.

Nasrudin's friend takes a cup of water and finds a dead fly in the water. He throws away the water, gets a new cup and fills it and drinks.

Nasrudin's donkey drinks from the bowl; there is a fly in the bowl, but the donkey drinks carefully and finishes the water and leaves the fly in the bowl.

Nasrudin lifts up his cup to drink and finds three flies in the cup. He carefully picks up the three flies with his fingers and squeezes them over the cup until every drop of water is back in the cup. He then throws the dry flies away and he drinks the water.

Then Nasrudin sings to himself:

He who minds the well knows
the value of water;
the donkey knows
it's best to save the master's wealth;
he who receives free, however,
wastes all that's offered

Note to children who may
be hearing this story

Do as your parents do – if they drink from
cups in which flies have fallen and if they
think you may do likewise, then be good
children and do as your parents say.
Do not use Nasrudin or his donkey as role
models in this regard.
Take Nasrudin's wisdom, and throw out the
flies.

Ask your parents what's the moral of this Nasrudin tale.

If what they tell you has anything to do with flies, then you can be sure they were donkeys in their previous births and are destined to be flies in the next.

Nasrudin's parrots

1
Nasrudin is in the town coffee-shop.
His donkey is tied to a pole outside the shop.

2
Nasrudin sits, drinking tea with a friend.
A man enters the coffee-shop and Nasrudin laughs
aloud.
Why are you laughing? asks Nasrudin's friend.

And Nasrudin says:
*Because this man talks like a parrot. Every time he
opens his mouth it's always the same subject: how his
job is the best in the world; and what he has done so
far…It's the same ideas in different words, always the
same thoughts…If you listened to him long enough,
you'd think he was a parrot…*

3
Then another man enters the coffee-shop. Again
Nasrudin bursts out laughing.
Why are you laughing? asks Nasrudin's friend.

And Nasrudin says:
*Because this man talks like a parrot. Every time he
opens his mouth it's always the same subject: he will
talk about all his travels; what countries he's been to;
what he ate there…and what he has seen so far…It's the*

same ideas in different words, always the same
thoughts…If you listened to him long enough, you'd
think he was a parrot…

4

A few minutes later, another man enters the coffee-shop.
Again Nasrudin bursts out laughing.
Why are you laughing now? asks Nasrudin's friend.

And Nasrudin says:
Because this man talks like a parrot. Every time he
opens his mouth it's always the same subject: he will
talk about his family; how his daughter is the cleverest
girl in the world; and how his son is doing very well at
school…and how well he brings them up…It's the same
ideas in different words – and always the same
thoughts…If you listened to him long enough, you'd
think he was a parrot…

5

And so Nasrudin sits there for about two hours, laughing
aloud at each person who enters the coffee-
shop…laughing at each person's parrot scripts…

6

Then Nasrudin says goodbye to his friend and goes out to his donkey.

The moment the donkey sees Nasrudin, it bursts out laughing.

It laughs so much it can't control itself, and it rolls on the ground, still laughing at Nasrudin.

Nasrudin waits patiently, and says to the donkey: *I know…I know…*

At last the donkey stops laughing, gets up, and takes Nasrudin home…

Nasrudin describes the world

1

Nasrudin is in his garden; his donkey is beside him.
Nasrudin's townsfolk come to see him. The crowd greets
Nasrudin.

Nasrudin, says one of the men in the crowd. *We do not
travel much. We do not have the time nor do we have
any interest in doing so. But we wonder often what lies
beyond our town.*
We want to know our world.

The others agree.
Nasrudin's donkey says: *Hee-haw! Hee-haw!*

What we would like you to do, Nasrudin, continues the
man, *is to climb to the top of the ancient tree on the town
hill. Climb right to the top and tell us what you see; and
so we will know what lies beyond our town. And so we
will come to know all about the world.*

The crowd agrees with the man. They all look at Nasrudin.
Will he do it? None of them dares to climb that ancient tall tree – as tall as if twenty men each stood on top of the other's head…

Hee-haw! Hee-haw! says the donkey.

Nasrudin pats his donkey. He turns to the crowd and says:
I will do it but my donkey wants to be there with me, right up at the top of the tree. My donkey wants me to sit on it and shout out the description to you. This is an important moment and my donkey wants to be there with me…

The crowd agrees.

2

And so the crowd prepares strong ropes and leather straps and huge tough blankets to haul Nasrudin's donkey up the tree.
The town gathers below the ancient tree on the hill.

First Nasrudin climbs up the tree, and after three hours of climbing, he is right up there at the top of the tree.
It looks like Nasrudin is sitting in the clouds.
He throws some ropes down over a huge trunk up far in the sky.

The townsfolk, using leather tongs and ropes and tough blankets, tie and secure the donkey to the ropes and then, pulling at the other end, they haul the donkey up to the branch where Nasrudin waits.

Two of the strongest men hold the ground end of the rope.

The crowd cheers as Nasrudin sits on his donkey.

The donkey says: *Hee-haw! Hee-haw!*

3

Nasrudin, in a clear voice, shouts to the townsfolk: *Are you ready to know all about the world?*

There is a roar of *YES!* from the crowd gathered below the tree.

And Nasrudin describes to the people what he sees*: I see the world all round our town.*

The crowd cheers with delight.

And Nasrudin continues:
I see valleys and mountains and hills all round our town.
There are many towns like ours.
I can see villages.
I can see people and animals moving.
I can see rivers like the one that runs through our town.
It is the same in the north; it is the same in the south and
the east, and in the west.
I have now described to you all that there is to be seen,
and all that is to be known.

Hee-haw! Hee-haw! says the donkey.

The crowd cheers.
Nasrudin gets off his donkey and climbs down the tree.
The crowd carefully brings the donkey down to the
ground.

4

When Nasrudin is on the ground, the crowd cheers
again.
They hug him and they are happy.

Then everyone is silent and one of the wisest of the
townsfolk speaks:
Nasrudin, today you and your donkey have done a great
thing for us.
You have gone up the tallest tree in our town and you
have described the world.

Through your eyes we have seen the world.
Through your words we have come to know all that
there is to be known about the world.
Through you and your donkey we have come to know the
world.
Thank you, Nasrudin!

And the crowd cheers.
And the wisest of the townsfolk strokes Nasrudin's
donkey and he says:
Thank you, donkey!

The crowd cheers again.
And they disperse.
And as each goes, they thank Nasrudin. They say to
Nasrudin:
Now we know the world, Nasrudin.

Thank you, Nasrudin - now I know everything about the
world.

Thank you Nasrudin – I shall memorize every word of
yours because you have told us about everything that is
to be known.

5

Now Nasrudin and the donkey stand alone below the tree on the hill.
Nasrudin looks at the donkey.
The donkey looks at Nasrudin.

The donkey says: *Hee-haw! Hee-haw!*

I know, says Nasrudin to his donkey. *I know. Come, let us go…*

Sir Nasrudin

1
The Elder from a town nearby comes to visit Nasrudin.
The Elder accompanies Nasrudin as Nasrudin goes about his day.

They ride through the town, each on his donkey.
The Elder sees that people of all ages and races greet Nasrudin readily and they talk happily to Nasrudin.

2

Nasrudin! shouts an old woman, and Nasrudin stops to
talk to the old woman.
A trader shouts and waves to Nasrudin: *Nasrudin!*
Nasrudin laughs and waves back.
A beggar waves to Nasrudin and says: *Nasrudin!*

And old men, and young men and women and all sorts
of people and all classes of people
shout: *Nasrudin!* - and they wave to him.

3

And they come to a field. Nasrudin gets off his donkey
and throws some grains to the ground and the birds
come and eat. And even the birds seem to cry out:
Nasrudin! Nasrudin! Nasrudin!

4

At last they come across a playground.
And the children stop their games and they shout:
Nasrudin! Nasrudin! Nasrudin!
And the children run to Nasrudin and he gives them
lollies he carries in a bag strapped to his donkey's back.
And the children shout: *Nasrudin – one for me! Me too,
Nasrudin! Don't forget me – Nasrudin!*
And then the children continue with their play.

The Elder turns to Nasrudin and says:
Nasrudin, all people love you and call you by your name. But how is it that these children also call you by name? They should call you 'Sir' or by a title of respect! I shall speak to them and admonish them now!

But Nasrudin holds the Elder gently by his arm and says:
Please, Sir – do not do that. When we all approach each other with love as fellow beings, what need is there for titles and salutations? Of all human beings the children are the ones who can sense love most – and that they call me by name and not by a title shows me the love they have for me.

Hee-haw !Hee-haw! says Nasrudin's donkey.

It is true, says the Elder.
From that day the Elder drops all titles.

Nasrudin sells crabs

1
Nasrudin sees that his townsfolk are lazy and jealous of
one another. Some do nothing all day and many are
jealous of those who work and become successful. Many
also conspire and seek to destroy one another.

Ah, says Nasrudin to his donkey, *I wish people will help
one another instead of being jealous and trying to
destroy others...*
And Nasrudin is silent. He is thinking…
And the donkey too thinks, and as it gets an idea it says:
Hee-haw! Hee-haw!

Nasrudin comes to the busy Sunday market.
His donkey carries three huge baskets.
Nasrudin and his donkey set up a stall.
He places the three baskets on a wooden table and sits
down on a chair.

2

The people in the market are excited.
What is Nasrudin selling? says one.
Nasrudin has never been here before, says another.
What is Nasrudin selling?

And the townsfolk gather at Nasrudin's stall.
Nasrudin, what are you selling? they ask.

Crabs! shouts Nasrudin.
Hee-haw! shouts the donkey.

Crabs? asks someone. May *we see them?*
And the donkey, tied to a post near Nasrudin, says*: Hee-haw! Hee-haw!*

3

And Nasrudin lifts the lid off the first basket.
There are crabs.
Oh, says one of the men. *What kind of crabs are these?
They move very slowly and their eyes are half-open and
they look sleepy...*

Ah, Nasrudin says, these *are the lazy crabs...They just
lie around and do nothing!*
Hee-haw! says the donkey.

And Nasrudin lifts the lid off the second basket.

4

And what about these crabs, Nasrudin? asks an old woman, pointing to the second basket. *They seem to be moving fast to and fro...and look...there's a crab over there that's trying to climb up – and the others are forming a sort of pile and the crab is now climbing on them, and is nearly reaching the rim of the basket...*

Nasrudin pushes the crab back in...
These crabs help one another fulfill their aspirations, he says.
Hee-haw! says the donkey.

And Nasrudin lifts the lid off the third basket.

5

And these, says a young man, *pointing to the crabs in the third basket, are very active too.*

Except, says another man, looking into the same basket, *this time, there's a crab that's climbing up and as soon as it does that, look, the others all rush to it and they then drag that crab down...Then there's another crab that tries to climb and then all the others rush to that crab and pull that crab down...This seems to be going on and on...What's happening here?*

And Nasrudin says:

These are crabs that will not allow any other crab fulfill its aspirations...they're jealous crabs that are out to drag down everyone else with them...

Hee-haw! says the donkey.

6

And now everyone has quite a lot of crabs to eat – and the town also has quite a bit of food for thought too...

Hee-haw! says the donkey. *Hee-haw! Hee-haw!*

Nasrudin: animal or human?

The philosopher approaches Nasrudin. And the philosopher explains what he does.
And then methodically, the philosopher asks Nasrudin:
Say, Nasrudin – are you animal or man?

Nasrudin gets off his donkey, ties the donkey to a post nearby and then he sits with the philosopher on the ground below a tree.

Say, Nasrudin – are you animal or man? asks the philosopher again.

When I am riding my donkey, and we act in harmony thus, and my donkey obeys – then I feel like I am part man and part animal. And perhaps my donkey too feels then part animal and part human.

And at other times?

When I answer these questions and my donkey can only chew grass, I feel human. But when my donkey looks at me after each answer I make, I feel like I'm just a donkey, providing silly answers...

And at other times?

When I eat and my donkey too eats, I feel like an animal. But when I eat cooked meat and sweetened bread, and food that is processed and changed and combined before I eat, I feel so human...

And at other times?

When it is evening, and my donkey retires to its shed to rest, and I go into my house and lie down on my mat to sleep, I feel like an animal...

And at other times?

When the politicians and the organizations and my relatives all come to put their claims on me, to warn me about my duties and obligations and what it means to be part of society, and what I must do and what I must not do, then I feel very human...
But at this moment, Sir, at this very moment, Sir, I feel like an animal because you are using me and working me too hard with all these questions...

The philosopher laughs and says:
But what would your conclusion be, Nasrudin? Are you animal or man?

And Nasrudin says:
But that is your job, Sir - for I have provided the data and information you seek and it is up to you to form conclusions. For in listening and not making conclusions, now, you would be an animal...

And the philosopher says:
Do you want to listen to my conclusions?

And Nasrudin says:
Stop Sir, for that will make us both human...and that is always a silly thing!

What's so funny, Nasrudin?

One evening, as usual, Nasrudin was having his tea at the town tea-shop.

Just then a very important-looking man walked in and sat opposite Nasrudin.
The man ordered his drink, scowled when the shop-assistant brought his tea to him, and threw his coins on the table for the shop-assistant to pick up.

Then this important-looking man continued to drink his tea, never smiling, never looking at anyone and maintaining a harsh expression on his face...

And Nasrudin laughed. Nasrudin laughed aloud...

What's so funny? shouted the important-looking man. *You must be laughing at me! What's so funny?*

And Nasrudin said:
Sir, there's absolutely nothing funny about you - that's why I laughed!

Nasrudin's donkey for sale

A buyer of animals says to Nasrudin:
I shall buy your donkey, Nasrudin.

Nasrudin says his donkey is not for sale but the buyer of animals persists and calls on Nasrudin on various occasions.

I shall buy your donkey, Nasrudin, says the buyer of animals again.

Will you buy a human? asks Nasrudin.

No, Nasrudin – I am not a dealer in slaves, says the buyer of animals.

And Nasrudin says to him:
How then can you buy a donkey, Sir – that is more human than animal than most humans are?

The magician and Nasrudin

Nasrudin sits at a table on the pavement just outside the coffee-shop in his small home-town. His donkey is tied to a post beside the shop.

A man, dressed in rainbow turban, walks to Nasrudin.

May I sit here with you, Sir? asks the man.

Nasrudin nods and smiles.

Sir, says the man, *you must be Nasrudin.*

Nasrudin smiles and nods. *I'm getting a bit too famous,* he thinks to himself, *and that's never good.*

Sir, the man continues loudly, *I'm passing through your town and I'm a famous magician. You may call me Magician.*

Never mind your fame, says Nasrudin, *but what do you do?*

Sir, says the man, let me explain. *Even as I sit here I can make to materialize right here before us, right here on this table, two cups of tea. Right now. I can do it.*

Nasrudin raises his right hand. A coffee-shop attendant comes running to Nasrudin. Nasrudin lifts his index finger to indicate one.

One cup of tea, Sir, says the coffee-shop attendant and runs off and, within seconds, is back with a steaming cup of tea. He places this on the table before Nasrudin. Nasrudin hands over half a coin to the attendant who leaves with a smile and a bow.

Nasrudin takes a sip of the tea, and he says to the Magician:
See, Mr Magician, without uttering a word I've produced a cup of tea, just for a half a copper coin. Now Sir Magician, work your magic – and even as we sit here, you can make to materialize right here before us, right here on this table, just one cup of tea, just for yourself. For I have mine. Go on sir, you can do it. Right now.

The Magician disappeared and was never heard of again.

A name for the donkey

Why, Nasrudin, my dear friend, asked a man one day,
have you not given your donkey a name?

And Nasrudin replied:
Why, what's wrong with donkey?

And yet the man asked again:
*But why not a name? My dear friend, Nasrudin. Tell me.
Why not give your donkey a name?*

And Nasrudin replied:

*We live in a dangerous world, my dear friend. If I should
give my donkey a specific name, and even if I should
give this name with love, and even if I should call this
donkey by the name I give most endearingly, there are
people in this world who will take offense for the
slightest reason and who may consequently want to
inflict the harshest punishment on me and on my donkey.
We live in such a world.*
*You know this, my friend. And yet you tell me this and
repeat I should give my donkey a name. Surely you
cannot be my friend when you know what kind of a
dangerous world we live in and when you repeat that I
should give my donkey a name?*

And Nasrudin's donkey, which was beside Nasrudin and
had been listening to this conversation said angrily: *Hee-
haw! Hee-haw!*

Nasrudin's simple moment

Nasrudin was away on a long journey. And when he returned, the people of his town came to see him. *Nasrudin,* said an elder. *Where have you been? What have you seen? What have you learned?*

And Nasrudin cleared his throat and he said:
I have been round the world these many years. With my faithful companion, the donkey, I have been to many lands and many countries and to mighty empires...

I saw Great Kings and dined with Emperors; I discoursed with mighty Generals and Conquerors and rode with their regiments and saw them conquer, plunder and bring countries down to their knees; I saw mighty palaces and buildings and great homes and great carriages; and immense cities and grand displays of power and pomp...

I witnessed lengthy festivities and celebrations and fireworks and loud displays of military might; and I saw the marvels of engineering and architecture and works of gargantuan proportions that civilizations display and boast....

I met mighty minds and intellects that could analyze Heaven and Hell, and solve all mysteries and offer solutions to every problem that irks humanity.

I discoursed with Giants in Various Fields of All Classified Knowledge and listened to their expositions of World Schemes and right and wrong and their Great

Discourses on Truth and Metaphysics... And I met and listened to all the Great Teachers and the World Philosophers and the anointed Prophets and Saviors; and I listened to all their orations on the Books that contain all Truth...

And I was at tables and Halls where the poets and the artists and the sculptors and the musicians and the geishas and concubines gathered; and also there were the dancers and the magicians and orators and the craftsmen, and all manner of beautiful people, all manner of inspired people who all displayed their skills and their Great Works and their Immortal Creations...

And I feasted on food and banquets that were the finest in each land; and I feasted at tables of food that stretched from the furthest street to the heart of the Palace...

And yet, yet, nothing could equal a quiet moment below a tree, just me and my donkey; nothing can equal a quiet moment below a tree, me and my donkey, just observing...just observing the beauty of a sunrise or a sunset, or just to see the stars and the moon...and to sip a little water from my own cup and to eat some simple bread...and share it with my companion, the donkey...and just to see the beauty of that simple moment... Nothing that I have seen or experienced or have been offered in all my travels is equal to that simple moment...Nothing can surpass a simple moment...

Nasrudin's end in the beginning

1

In the days when Nasrudin was but a young man, he
spent much time resting and lazing below the trees
beside the river.
His donkey would sit on the ground beside him, or walk
around the trees or even down the river, though always
careful to keep its master within sight…

But Nasrudin, he would simply lie there, listening to the
birds, or to the breeze whistling in the trees…Or he
would sit up and gaze at the sunset and the sunrise, and
the gentle light that fell on the river before him…

And thus he spent many days of his youth…

2

One day, a group of five men walked round the area
where Nasrudin and his donkey were resting.

The five men walked to and fro, pointed to the other side
of the river, and then walked around again, stopping to
point at the ground and then pointing across the river...
Then they seemed to have finished whatever it was that
they were doing...

They stood in a group now and looked at Nasrudin and
his donkey.

Nasrudin and his donkey ignored them...Nasrudin lay
on the ground with a cloth over his eyes; and his donkey
lay near him, chewing some grass...Nasrudin could hear
the gentle waves of the water breaking against the
pebbles that lay at the edge of the river...

3

Then the five men walked to where Nasrudin was.

Hello, young man, said one of the men who was rather portly, well-dressed and important looking.
Hello, young man, he said again, when Nasrudin did not answer.

*Hm....*said Nasrudin lazily.

What's your name, young man? said the portly man.

Nasrudin, came the reply.

Ah, Nasrudin, said the portly man. *I have bought the lands on this side of the river and on the other side too. My friends and I are going to run a ferry service so people can cross the river safely...We are going to build shops on either side and we are also going to build inns so that people can rest while on a journey...But what are you doing here, young man?*

*Lying down below the tree; enjoying life...enjoying nature...*said Nasrudin.

4

Ah, Nasrudin, said the portly man. *That is a waste of time. That is what you are doing.*
Just wasting time...I'll tell you what you should be doing, Nasrudin.

What's that? said Nasrudin.
Hee-haw? said the donkey, which was by now sitting up and paying attention to the portly man.

5

You should stop being lazy and get up, Nasrudin, said the portly man.

And then? said Nasrudin.
Hee-haw? the donkey joined in.

And then get a job, continued the portly man.
And then? asked Nasrudin.
And then get a big fat monthly pay.
And then?
Hee-haw?
And go and save your money.
And then?
Hee-haw?
Well, save enough and buy a house…
And then?
Hee-haw?
And after that, get a better job… earn more money…
And then?
Hee-haw?
With so much wealth, it'll be time to get married…look for a nice woman, and get married…
And then?
Hee-haw?
Well, have a few kids…
And then?
Hee-haw?
Bring them up to be responsible people…

And then?
Hee-haw?
Get them married...
And then?
Hee-haw?
*Continue working and making money...buy one or two
more properties...*
And then?
Hee-haw?
Then you might really be very rich...
And then?
Hee-haw?
*And then you may not even need to work...and so you
can retire...*
And then?
Hee-haw?
*And then – well, you retire – and all you have to do is
just relax, lie down at home; just relax and enjoy your
life!*

But you, fool! - said Nasrudin. *That's what I'm doing
right now! Why should I do all that you say, and go
through all that trouble to relax and enjoy my life –
when I can do that right now, right in the beginning -
without all that effort!?*

Hee-haw! Hee-haw! Hee-haw! Hee-haw! Hee-haw!

And thus did Nasrudin first gain his reputation as a
fool...

Nasrudin: gone star-seeing

Once, while on their travels, Nasrudin and his donkey
stopped to rest a day or two at one of the little towns of
Surapur.
The King of Surapur heard of Nasrudin's sojourn and
immediately sent a royal messenger to deliver Nasrudin
a letter of invitation.

The King's letter to Nasrudin read as follows:

Most renowned Nasrudin.

It gives us great pleasure that you should have stopped at a town in our kingdom.

Three nights from now our capital city will be the venue for the largest fireworks display ever hosted by any monarch. This royal display will be so magnificent the fireworks will be visible a hundred miles from our grand city.

The fireworks will include glorious displays in the sky of fire shapes of flowers, people's faces, and all sorts of geometric shapes.

It is our pleasure to invite you to this display. A special seat will be reserved for you in the Pavilion of Radiance for honored guests of the City.

It will give the City great pleasure to have you as a guest at the royal Fireworks Display.
Kindly be ready early in the morning and you will be transported to the city in one of our royal chariots.

And Nasrudin sent a reply back to the king:

Your Highness...Thank you for your invitation but my donkey and I must decline your invitation.

My donkey prefers nature's majestic display of the stars in the night sky, and its glorious display of grass and flowers in the morning fields.

And thus, tomorrow, we shall depart far north to the Tara fields of grass and flowers; and on in the evening to the Sora fields – well over two hundred miles away from your City, to view the night's display of the stars above Sora fields...

Forgive me, Sire, but the donkey rules on such matters...The donkey, not being human, is closer to nature and to its instinct than humans are, and will not listen to any reason.

And thus the donkey and I will be away to the Tara fields and then to the Sora fields...

Nasrudin moves in

Monday – When Nasrudin and his family returned home in the evening, they found their garden furniture missing.

Tuesday - Nasrudin and his family found their Persian carpet in the living room missing.

Wednesday – Nasrudin hid himself in his store room and saw his neighbor Izumudin steal his antique chairs.

Thursday - Izumudin returned to his own home with Nasrudin's teak table.
But when he opened the door to his house, he found Nasrudin, Nasrudin's wife and children sitting and laughing in the living room.

Nasrudin! shouted Izumudin. *What are you and your family doing in my house?*

And Nasrudin said: *Oh, we accepted your invitation and just moved in!*

Confused, Izumudin shouted: *What are you talking about? I never invited you to move in here!*

And Nasrudin said:
Oh you've moved all our things here to your house so we knew you were inviting us to move in to your house!
We've already finished all the food you had in the kitchen. Now have you thought about what we are going to have for dinner?

Nasrudin's sinking ship

Nasrudin was at the coffee-shop and a man with an inquiring mind asked Nasrudin many questions.

One of the most inquiring questions the man asked of Nasrudin was:
If you were on a ship, Nasrudin, and the ship sunk, and you were the only survivor to be stranded on a deserted island, which one book would you take with you?

And Nasrudin said:
I would not take a book; I would not take any book, my dear friend – I should take all the preserved meat and all the food I can lay my hands on...But then if I knew all that you say would happen, I would not even be on that ship!

Nasrudin is right!

The local justice of peace went away to the City for a few months. So Nasrudin was called in to judge a case.

First the accuser made a loud and fierce declamatory speech against the accused.
Then the accuser sat down.
Nasrudin looked at the accuser and he said: *You're right.*

 Then the accused stood up and delivered an impassioned and eloquent speech on his innocence.
Then the accused sat down.
Nasrudin looked at the accused and he said: *You're right.*

Someone jumped up and shouted: *Nasrudin! How can two people with contradictory views both be right?*

You're also right! retorted Nasrudin

And the accuser and the accused stood up and they said to each other:
Nasrudin is right; let's settle this between ourselves -
and they did so amicably, and hugged each other and went their separate ways in peace.

And someone said: *Nasrudin – you're right!*

Nasrudin: number one

(the following translation from the original Silence is provided by Raj Arumugam; translation of the Donkey language is by Nasrudin himself, with very minor deletions of unflattering remarks by the donkey)

One fine morning, as he was getting ready to go to the Great City, Nasrudin was seized by ambition.

He said to his donkey: *I want to be Number One.*

The donkey looked at Nasrudin and said:
I thought you were human. Why do you want to be a number?

Nasrudin: some lunacies

If humans were donkeys and donkeys were human, then we wouldn't have any idiocy, would we?

If men were women and women were men, than we'd just have a different set of problems, wouldn't we?

If the earth were the moon, and the moon were the earth, we wouldn't have all this lunacy, would we?

If no one had any more children, and so if there are no more children coming into this world, then all our problems in the world would gradually end, wouldn't they?

If I were you, and you were Nasrudin, there'd still be a fool, wouldn't there?

If you were the Highest Authority in your land, because you have become the Highest Authority in the land, there'd still be corruption and all the evils in your land, wouldn't there?

If I were my donkey and my donkey were Nasrudin, then we'd still have a donkey and we'd still have a Nasrudin. Though one may not be as charming, and one not so witty...

Nasrudin talks to his donkey

INTRODUCTION

Nasrudin and his donkey talk to each other often. They treat each other as friends and they talk.

Nasrudin shares his thoughts with his donkey; and his donkey hee-haws to indicate agreement or disagreement.

Sometimes the donkey hee-haws to put forth a question. And Nasrudin answers part in human language and part in donkey language...

They understand each other.

The following are excerpts from some of the conversations between the donkey and Nasrudin. (The donkey language was translated by Nasrudin.)

Warning to human beings and donkeys

Human beings may find the following material offensive.

Donkeys may find that the following material may only give rise to donkey-complacency…So please, when your masters read this to you, listen with your thinking caps on…

Donkey, my loyal donkey…

*

Enjoy life, donkey. I don't know how donkeys enjoy life, but I'm sure you donkeys too have a way of enjoying life. Find your way and enjoy life.

I know you work like a donkey – well, pardon the expression – but look, we human beings too work like donkeys, pardon the expression again.
But each, whether human or donkey, whatever our circumstances, must find a way to find happiness and to enjoy life.
No one else can do it for you: it's that simple. Enjoy your life and find your own happiness.

Hee-haw! Hee-haw!

*

Ah, donkey...you complain you'd rather be human and not be a donkey – then, you say, then you might be able to ride an animal and be as free as humans...

But then human beings too can become beasts of burden: they can be conquered by other countries or they can be lorded over by their own Generals and Leaders and Politicians and Spouses...
That's the obvious sort of burden that can be imposed on them: but they can rise and fight and throw away those burdens – but there's another sort of burden in which human beings are truly donkeys – pardon that expression, dear donkey...

Hee-haw! Hee-haw!

Yes, yes, donkey, you are right; they can fight against that burden and be free...
You are right, donkey – but you are right only to a certain extent...the problem with human existence is that humans are almost never free...they are often willing slaves to one thing or another: they are slaves to habits; they are slaves to superstitions, to words their ancestors left them centuries ago, to books and to Imagined Beings; they are slaves to their own Big Lies about a Big Mean Pig Being who lives and watches over them; they are slaves to traditions, and to all sorts of institutions and human encumbrances...all their lives they are slaves, donkey – and the funny thing is that in most cases they never know they are slaves...how happy then to be a donkey because you know you have a master and know

*you are owned by someone - but poor humans, they
never know who owns them and how they are controlled
and what patterns and systems drive them...
And the worse thing, donkey, the worse thing is they go
around thinking they are such clever beings – when in
fact they are just beasts of burden; ignorant they are
born, and ignorant they die...they are the true donkeys –
oh my beloved donkey, pardon the expression...*

Hee-haw! Hee-haw!

*

Hee-haw! Hee-haw! Hee-haw! Hee-haw!

*Ah yes, dear donkey...human intelligence...yes, we
probably appear hugely intelligent and so you think the
human condition is vastly superior to that of a
donkey's...no, no – that's very true, dear donkey...we
humans spend our days and nights like donkeys, pardon
the expression, dearest donkey – but it's true... though
humans are endowed with brains and intelligence – we
do not use these gifts...*

*The day human beings are born, the parents take over
their brains and later they hand over these brains to the
teachers who take it from there – and do you think we
human beings ever get to use our brains? – no, because
the brains always belong to somebody else; humans are
truly like donkeys, pardon the expression; and just as a
donkey's body and time is completely at the disposal of
the master – these donkey-humans have all their minds*

*and brains, and intelligence and their lives completely
taken over by others...therefore are they human-
donkeys...it is worse than being a donkey...*

*And do you think the parents and teachers and society
have a brain or intelligence of their own? No,
everyone's handed it over to somebody or something
else...*

*Oh, all we have are donkeys, but pardon that expression,
dear donkey...*

Hee-haw! Hee-haw!

*

Hee-haw! Hee-haw!

*Ah, dearest donkey...you are wise...you are wise...yes,
that's the reason why I live so much outside
society...yes, yes, you have observed me correctly...yes,
by pretending to be a mad man, by pretending to be
unwise, by pretending not to understand things, and by
living my life mostly outside society I have gained my
independence...Yes, this way, I'm less encumbered than
the other donkeys; yes, yes – ha! ha! – you are right –
I'm also a donkey but I'm less of a donkey than the
others because at least I get to keep my brains ...ha! ha!
– you're clever for a donkey – ooops! Sorry about
that...yes...yes...so I just admire the flowers and do my
part and do my thing; I keep things simple and enjoy life
and yes, in such ways, I find my independence and
freedom – in such ways I get to keep my brains and I*

have a mind of my own...yes, yes...each must find one's
own way...
Ah, you're clever for a donkey...I'm sorry, sorry...I shall
not say that again...
But yes, you enjoy your life, given all the restrictions,
and I too have found my own way to enjoy my life, given
all the restrictions and constraints...we do our best; and
that's all that matters...that we'll be dust one day,
knowing we did the good thing...that we each lived a life
of being more than a donkey...all right, all right, pardon
the expression...

Hee-haw! Hee-haw!

Donkey, ah my loyal donkey...eat your food, rest well
and be strong – for tomorrow you'll have to carry me
miles and miles...
Donkey, ah my loyal donkey...

POSTSCRIPT

Hee-haw! Hee-haw? Hee-haw! Hee-haw?

Ah ,what is it, dear donkey? Have I ever shared these
thoughts with my fellow human beings? Oh, no – never,
dear donkey. For if I shared these thoughts with
my fellow human beings, they may be offended and may
beat me like a cruel master beats his donkey...

*No, I will not speak these thoughts...let my fellow human
beings think of me as a fool – that's safer; and therefore
I say it is wise to be a fool and it is foolish to be wise.*

*But perhaps one day some fool will come along and put
these conversations down for others to read...ah, that
poor fool...*

Nasrudin at the river

This stranger stands on the rocky side of the river.
He wants to get to the other side of the river.
He tests the water and realizes that it is as deep as it is
wide.
He can't swim.

There's not even a boat or a boatman in sight! he
mutters to himself. *The people of this area must
be stupid! Why don't they build a bridge or run a ferry
service?*

As he stands fretting and cursing, Nasrudin appears on the other side of the river.
Nasrudin is riding his donkey.

Hey! You on the donkey! shouts the man to Nasrudin.

Yes, Sir...can I help you? shouts back Nasrudin.

Yes, tell me how I can get to the other side of the river! shouts the man.

And the answer comes from Nasrudin, loud and clear:
But Sir, as far as I can see, you are already on the other side of the river!

And Nasrudin shakes his head, and rides away and he tells his donkey:
These foreigners...for some reason, they're always stupid!

Nasrudin meets the philosopher

A man came to see Nasrudin.
I'm a philosopher, he declared to Nasrudin.
What's that? asked Nasrudin.

Philosophers, you might say, deal with the pursuit of human happiness.

Human happiness? said Nasrudin, puzzled. *So my donkey has no place in your world?*

No, no you don't understand, said the philosopher. *Animals, except perhaps in captivity, are naturally happy; human beings have to seek happiness. So philosophy is the pursuit of human happiness.*

Nasrudin considered that for a while and then he said: *Then you may continue pursuing it and happiness will continue evading you.*

How's that? asked the philosopher.

Well, let's see, said Nasrudin. *Are you perfect?*

No, said the philosopher. *No one is perfect.*

So you are imperfect, said Nasrudin.

Certainly, said the philosopher.

If you are imperfect you are filled with contradictions, said Nasrudin. *And anything filled with contradiction is imperfect.*

Yes, you could say so. Though in my case I try and minimize my contradictions but still I am contradictory.

So as a human being you are contradictory?

Yes, I am, agreed the philosopher.

To be contradictory, said Nasrudin, *is to be filled with tension and friction. To be contradictory is to be filled with tension within oneself and within society.*

The philosopher said: *Yes, indeed.*

And Nasrudin continued:
And to be filled with contradictions and tension, my dear friend, that is always to be unhappy. So you will never find happiness – so the pursuit of happiness is a useless profession. So, my dear friend, go home, forget about this pursuit of happiness and drink your chicken soup - and be happy!

The philosopher did so and he was happy. From then he was no longer a philosopher; he was a happy man.

Nasrudin, *the musical*

Nasrudin, *the musical*

Introduction

it's a van Gogh day
in evergreen spring
and the morning dances
like a maiden with flowers
blossoms in her hair
and round her waist
round her neck and wrists;
oh she's so fresh and corpulent
singing with red, red lips

and on this bunny sunny day
Nasrudin and his dog
(well it's a donkey we know
but 's so faithful
one may call it a dog anyway)
and so Nasrudin and his donkey
are out on a ride
down the streets, 'cross the deserts
and across the fields
and into the horizon and
far straight, when possible,
straight into the heart of the sun

and there they go
Nasrudin
and his donkey-dog;
and as they ride
on these happy fields -
say do you know what they sing?

ha ha ha
he he he
ho ho ho
ha ho he!

hee-haw haw
hee-haw haw
he he he
hee-haw ho

ha ha ha
hee-haw haw
ho ho ho
hee-haw ho

when the mind's bitter
and the heart's heavy
when the eyes are dull
and time's 'r hard
and the days trying -
you know
all you have to do
is to sing and dance
like Nasrudin
and his simple beast:
ha ha ha

he he he
ho ho ho
ha ho he!

so your wife's not home
and dinner's not done?
Or your hubby's out
and 's sure to come home drunk;
or your son's gone out in the night
and turned off his darned mobile!
and your daughter's gone to dance school
but her teacher's not seen her
since six lessons ago!
O you know
all you have to do then
is to sing and dance
like Nasrudin
and his simple beast:
 hee-haw haw
hee-haw haw
he he he
hee-haw ho

Oh all right
everything's just too good
and all things perfect;
got the sweetest spouse possible
and kids are just angels;
your fortune's made
and money builds, grows and flows;
and you just work for fun and pleasure
and yet all of this 's not made you happy

just more boredom
and angst
and more kleptomania;
then, my dear,
all you have to do
is to sing and dance
like Nasrudin
and his simple beast:
ha ha ha
hee-haw haw
ho ho ho
hee-haw ho

ah it's a van Gogh day
in evergreen spring
and the morning dances
like a maiden with flowers
blossoms in her hair
and round her waist
and round her neck and wrists;
oh she's so fresh and corpulent
singing with red, red lips
and she sings aloud this way:

ha ha ha
he he he
ho ho ho
ha ho he!

hee-haw haw
hee-haw haw
he he he
hee-haw ho

149

ha ha ha
hee-haw haw
ho ho ho
hee-haw ho

Do you too, sweethearts, donkeys and all humans – do you too join in…enough of your whisperings and winging and darkness, and paranoid moodiness and complaints. Just sing and be happy:

all humans sing!
ha ha ha
he he he
ho ho ho
ha ho he!

now all donkeys sing!
hee-haw haw
hee-haw haw
he he he
hee-haw ho

and humans and donkeys together now!
ha ha ha
hee-haw haw
ho ho ho
hee-haw ho

marvelous, all beasts and humans! you are all so adorable! Love and lots of hee-haw!

Song of Nasrudin and his donkey

woke up this morning
hearing in my head
the song of Nasrudin
and his loyal beast

ha ha ha
he he he
ho ho ho
ha ho he!

no time for darkness
no space for worries
just heaps of
joy and brightness

hee-haw haw
hee-haw haw
he he he
hee-haw ho

no time for darkness
no space for worries
just heaps of
joy and brightness

woke up this morning
hearing in my head
the song of Nasrudin
and his loyal beast

all humans sing!
ha ha ha
he he he
ho ho ho
ha ho he!

now all donkeys sing!
hee-haw haw
hee-haw haw
he he he
hee-haw ho

and all humans and donkeys together now!
ha ha ha
hee-haw haw
ho ho ho
hee-haw ho

marvelous, all beasts and humans! you are all
so adorable! love and lots of hee-haw!

Donkey sings to its donkey friends

*Donkeys, unlike human beings, have no sense
of love for their fellow creatures. They have no
sense of gentleness or tenderness and again,
unlike us humans, they certainly have no sense
of irony.*
*Donkeys are donkeys, just as humans are
humans – as this donkey song proves, beyond
the donkey shadow of a doubt.*

1
donkey's inspiration

time has passed, dear donkey friends
and we have all drifted apart;
I stand often on the hilltop
and survey alone the world;
and though not a donkey is in sight
I remember all of you,
all my darling braying donkey friends;
I remember each and see you as clearly
as I see cacti and rocks in the sunlight
O dearest donkey friends all close to my heart
here is a song I hear often whispered to me
as I stand alone on this hilltop

2
sssh! - donkey sings

Ho friends
Hee-haw friends -
Somu and Muthu and Lila
and Peter and Lim and Hassan -
O noble donkeys all
dearest childhood friends -
each name evoking so much
love and fond memories -
are you all guys and gals still out there kicking
or each happily dead and blissfully gone
and practically eaten by worms and flies?

I remember how delightfully we played
running and hee-hawing and jumping
on hilltops and barren lands
and kicking dust and kicking arse
and pissing on cabbage plots -
a lot of horseplay, as the expression goes:
and so are you out there still kicking and alive
or are you gentle guys and gals all dead and gone?
and all heads and private parts all eaten
by resident worms and
by very patient flies?

I remember the days of youth
and the wonderful days at Donkey School
how they taught us obedience and to fit in into our roles
our masters had prepared for us;
to bear heavy loads all our lives
and to carry people's arses on our backs:
so are all you guys and gals
still out there scratching lines on sand?
and admiring your trophies for Best Support Roles?
or did you drop dead with your burdens
at last all happily dead and blissfully gone?

I remember how we each ate rationed dishes of hay
and a bucket of mixed salads
and to take care of our teeth
the occasional carrot;
and on special days
our proud masters decorated us
with leather harness and brilliant colors:
O are you out there still eating well
or each dead on too much of fatty stuff?
and perhaps now, dead and gone,
your jawbones decorate some barbarian's home?

Ho friends
Hee-haw friends -
Somu and Muthu and Lila
and Peter and Lim and Hassan -
O noble donkeys all
dearest childhood friends -
each name evoking so much
love and fond memories -
are you all guys and gals still out there kicking
or each happily dead and blissfully gone
and practically eaten by worms and flies?

The Nasrudin stories

Ah, I remember many things about Nasrudin... I remember as if they happen right here before my eyes...some events appear as if they are in the distant past – and yet some as if happening even now, right before my very eyes...

Nasrudin's donkey eats poetry

Nasrudin looks in the magic mirror that allows him to peep into the future and he sees many marvelous poems in cyberspace.

So Nasrudin calls his donkey and he says to the donkey:
See, donkey – there are so many marvelous poems in cyberspace. They are beautiful poems.

But Nasrudin's donkey says:
Ah what's the use? As far as I'm concerned the only good poem is the one printed on paper.

And why is that? asks Nasrudin.

Because at least when I'm desperately hungry I can eat paper – but I can't eat cyberspace can I? replies the donkey.

Nasrudin meets the Prince of Rome

This story recounts how, in ancient times, Nasrudin and his donkey met the Mighty Prince of Rome.

Nasrudin's donkey goes berserk with fear

In one of his travels, riding his faithful and hardy donkey to distant lands, Nasrudin met the Prince of Rome.
And this is how it happened.

Once, Nasrudin was riding through an unknown town. Suddenly, hearing the sound of trumpets and drums and the noise of soldiers marching and training, and seeing huge banners and insignias and a vast garrison of soldiers, his donkey bolted.
It became so afraid and senseless that it ran into what it feared: right into the streets where the soldiers were marching.

And the soldiers on horses chased Nasrudin and his donkey and shouted: *Stop! Stop!*

And yet, so afraid was the donkey, it ran right into the tent where the Prince of Rome was having his afternoon nap; and the soldiers standing guard there shouted at Nasrudin: *Stop in the name of the mighty Prince of Rome!* – and yet the donkey jumped over the Prince of Rome and ran on and on...

Nasrudin and his donkey are dragged into the presence of the Prince of Rome

Finally, a group of Roman soldiers stopped the donkey and arrested Nasrudin and the donkey, and dragged both them and brought them before the Prince of Rome.

One of the generals shouted at Nasrudin:
Know you not who this is? This is the mighty Prince of Rome! How dare you run through his tent and not stop when you and your donkey saw the mighty Prince of Rome!
You shall be flogged, you slave!

The Prince of Rome in turn glared at Nasrudin, and he roared: *Who are you, you dirty beggar with that scrawny-looking donkey?*

And on hearing these words the donkey brayed loudly: *Hee-haw! Hee-haw!* – as if to protest vehemently – not at the poor treatment of Nasrudin, but at the ignominy of being called a *scrawny-looking donkey*!

Speak, slave! said the Prince of Rome, staring curiously at the haughty donkey.

And Nasrudin said:
I am Nasrudin, O mighty Prince of Rome! I kneel before your might, O great Prince! I submit to your mercy, O mighty Prince of Rome!

The Prince of Rome was pleased with these words and he said: *I have heard of you Nasrudin. Stand up.*

And when Nasrudin stood up, the Prince of Rome said: *Why did you not stop when you were asked to? You seem to respect my power just then but why did you not stop when my soldiers ordered you to stop?*

And Nasrudin said:
Sir – I am human and I respect the power and authority of the land. But my donkey Sir, my donkey has no regard for power and authority and Princes and Kings and Emperors! It has no sense of what is right and what is wrong: It eats when it likes; and it releases flatulence when it likes! Why, it wouldn't even listen to me when I ordered it to stop!

And the soldiers laughed and the Prince of Rome laughed and the donkey went about in circles, braying happily: *Hee-haw! Hee-haw!*

And the Prince of Rome said:
Ah, Nasrudin – you are indeed wise; you are indeed the great teacher everyone says you are. You have taught me today a great lesson about life and pride and vanity.

And then the Prince of Rome ordered a feast in honor of Nasrudin and his donkey, and when the master and the donkey had eaten and rested well, the Prince sent them off on their journey with gold coins to last them for a year of travel.

And the Prince of Rome caused his scribes to have this meeting inscribed on a metal plate and to mount the plate up on the walls of the Town Hall; and even today if one should go to the ancient town of Nasputra , one may read this record.

But as it may not be convenient for all to travel to Nasputra, a translation of the text of the plate has been provided below on the royal command of the current mighty Prince of Rome:

Hee-haw! Hee-haw!

And thus was the happy meeting between the Prince of Rome Sr, and Nasrudin and his donkey.

Nasrudin tells a story

The donkey says to Nasrudin: *Tell me a short story.*

Nasrudin says: *OK. I've got a short story for you: There was once a man.*

The donkey says to Nasrudin: *You fool! Aristotle says a story must have a beginning, a middle and end!*

And Nasrudin says:
All right. I'll give you a story with a beginning, middle and an end.
Here it is: A man was born; he lived; he died!

And the donkey says: *That's better. At least it's got a beginning, a middle and an end!*

And Nasrudin says:

But so does the story: There was once a man. That is a story for those capable of subtlety; but 'A man was born; he lived; he died' is a story for the simpleminded. That's why you are a donkey, and I'm Nasrudin!

Nasrudin meets a goose

Nasrudin rides his donkey.
He thinks to himself: *Hm...the world is so old there is nothing surprising at all. There is nothing new and it's all getting so stale...*

 He sees a stray goose coming up his way from the opposite end of the street.
The goose comes closer, and as it passes him it looks up and says:
Good morning, Nasrudin. Good morning, donkey.

Hee-haw! says the donkey.
Good morning goose, says Nasrudin.

And then, thinking about the goose, Nasrudin says aloud to himself:
I didn't know geese could talk!

And Nasrudin's donkey says:
Neither did I.

A day in the life of Nasrudin and his donkey

Nasrudin rides his donkey.
Hee-haw! says the donkey.
Hee-haw! replies Nasrudin.
And thus they enjoy each other's company and engage in a conversation.

They pass a coffee-shop in the town marketplace.
By now of course the donkey is tired – as you probably know, even donkeys get tired.
So they enter the town with the donkey riding Nasrudin.

Hey Nasrudin, put that donkey down and come and join us for an intellectual discussion on the meaning of meaning! shouts a highly-intellectual-looking man.
So Nasrudin puts the donkey down. The donkey then goes to the coffee-shop for donkeys and Nasrudin joins the intellectual-looking man at the coffee-shop strictly for intellectuals.
(Yes, sadly even in those days, you could be the best of friends, but discrimination was indiscriminately and widely practiced.)

So Nasrudin finishes his intellectual discussion on the meaning of meaning and the donkey finishes whatever donkeys do in the pubs for donkeys, and man and donkey meet again and they ride again. Who carries who depends on who is more drunk after all those words.

Now they pass a playground. The children are playing happily.
Hey, Nasrudin, come and play! shout the children. *You can be the scarecrow and we'll throw little pebbles at you to scare the birds away!*
And so Nasrudin joins them and he stands like a scarecrow, and the children throw little pebbles at Nasrudin to scare away the birds and every time a pebble hits Nasrudin, the donkey goes*: Hee-haw! Hee-haw!*

And then the donkey and Nasrudin and the children play on the swings and they roll in the dust and the sands, and they play hide and seek…and now everyone is tired…it's time to go home…
Nasrudin rides on his donkey.
Hee-haw! says the donkey.
Hee-haw! replies Nasrudin.
And thus they enjoy each other's company and engage in a conversation.
Now they are on their way home, and as usual, they will each carry the other at least half way.

It's all just another day in the life of Nasrudin and his donkey.

Nasrudin returns from the Imperial City

1

Nasrudin went away to the Imperial City, the City Of Glories Beyond Compare.

When he returned to his town, everyone looked at Nasrudin as if he were some royal personage.

Nasrudin has been to the Imperial City! everyone shouted.

The old women stood on either side of the streets and they looked at Nasrudin riding his donkey through the streets, and they said: *He's been to the City of Glories!*

And Nasrudin held his head high, and his donkey looked very haughty indeed.

And the tradesmen and the workers and the merchants too came out and lined the streets and they said: *Wow! Look at Nasrudin. He has just come back from the Imperial City.*

Everyone came out to the streets to look in wonder at Nasrudin.

And the donkey brayed louder than it had ever done in its life: *HEE-HAW! HEE-HAW!*

2

And later that evening the merchants gathered at the Town Inn of Exotic Dinners and organized a sumptuous dinner in honor of Nasrudin. They invited Nasrudin to sit at the seat of honor at the table and the merchants made many speeches, praising Nasrudin for having visited the Imperial City.

And at this dignified event, after Nasrudin had eaten as much as he had liked, the merchants had many questions for Nasrudin about his visit to the Grand City.

Nasrudin! shouted a merchant.
Please do not shout! admonished Nasrudin very calmly. *Shouting reveals your provincial origin. It is cultured to speak softly.*

And everyone agreed. *See, Nasrudin has been to the City of Splendor and he is cultured. Treat him accordingly. Please speak softly to Nasrudin*!

And so the aforementioned merchant spoke softly and he asked very courteously:
Please, Nasrudin. Did you meet the Emperor?

Yes, said Nasrudin, hardly looking at the merchant.

There was a murmur of excitement, but which was quickly suppressed by the gathering's newly acquired learning that cultured people do not display excitement.

Another merchant in the gathering asked with great dignity: *Honored Nasrudin - having met the Emperor, did you also speak with the Emperor?*

Nasrudin cast a contemptuous look at the merchant and he said: *Of course, I did!*

There was great silence. Everyone was in awe of Nasrudin, at this man who had not only met the Emperor but had even spoken with the Emperor of the City of Great Splendor.

And what, O Most Honored Nasrudin, what did the Emperor say to you? asked a merchant most sheepishly.

Get out of my way, you imbecile! - that's what the Emperor said to me.
Oh, I assure you, continued Nasrudin, *though he is the Emperor of the City of Glories Beyond Compare, he is the crudest man alive! I was just riding my donkey and admiring the buildings in the streets when the Emperor*

was there with his entourage and he screamed at me:
Get out of my way, you imbecile!
Would you ever shout at a visitor to our town in that
manner? Oh, the Emperor is the rudest man I have ever
met!
Get out of my way, you imbecile! - that's all he
could say!

Nasrudin's hat, coat, and shoes

the invitation

Ah, how happy Nasrudin is!
See, he's just received an invitation from Amir, his very rich friend.

Waving the invitation in the air, Nasrudin says: *Amir is not just my friend. He's a very rich man! He's not just a very rich man, he's the richest in the city! And to think I have an invitation from him to join him and his friends for dinner tomorrow! Ah, I'm so fortunate! But you're not invited!*
And he waves the invitation at his donkey.
The donkey brays: *Hee-haw! Hee-haw!*
Oh, you're so disagreeable! says Nasrudin.

Nasrudin gets ready

It's the next day.
Nasrudin gets ready to go to his friend's house for dinner.
Ah, see how excited Nasrudin is.
He puts on his old clothes, and his torn sandals, and admires himself in the mirror.
The world respects a clever man and that's why I'm invited, he says.

The donkey, standing outside and looking in through the window, brays:
Hee-haw! Hee-haw!

Oh, you're so disagreeable! says Nasrudin. *And you're not coming because you're not invited!*

Nasrudin arrives outside Amir's home

Nasrudin walks to Amir's house and arrives at the gate.
See how many important proud faces and arrogant legs
walk into the mansion.

*And I have been invited, poor though I am, for my
wisdom*, Nasrudin thinks to himself.
And as he thinks to himself, he can almost hear his
donkey braying in his mind:
Hee-haw! Hee-haw!

And so Nasrudin arrives at the gates of his friend's
house.
Stop there! the guards shout at Nasrudin.
Nasrudin stops. He is shocked.

And one of the guards screams at Nasrudin: *Where do
you think you are going? Get out of here.*
And Nasrudin shows the guards the invitation and the
guards laugh.
One of the guards says to him:
*Look at all these visitors going in. See how well-dressed
they are. My master is so rich, do you think he would
invite a man like you? You look so miserable! Now go
away from here!*

Poor Nasrudin. He protests but it's no use. The guards
won't let him in. He walks back home.

The moment he reaches home his donkey brays: *Hee-
haw! Hee-haw!*
Oh shut up, says Nasrudin to the donkey. *You are so
disagreeable.*

But Nasrudin is a wise man. Or at least he likes to think of himself as being one.

He has an idea. He'll get past those guards yet.

He puts on the only rich hat he has. He puts on a colorful coat. And he puts on the only pair of leather shoes he owns.

And now he returns to Amir's house.

And this time the guards check his invitation and let him in.

They say to Nasrudin: *Welcome sir to our master's home - and they whisper to themselves: He must be an important man from another country. His clothes are very different.*

dinner is served

Amir and his guests including Nasrudin are now seated for dinner.
There is much laughter and happiness, and there is so much food placed before them.
Please, all my guests, please eat, says Amir.
And everyone starts to eat. The food is so delicious no one talks.

But Nasrudin does not eat.
He takes off his coat.
He takes off his shoes. He takes off his hat.
Now people stop eating and they look at Nasrudin's strange behavior.

Even Amir has stopped eating and is looking at Nasrudin.

Then Nasrudin takes his hat, and puts it into the soup and he says: *Drink, hat! Drink!*
And Nasrudin takes his shoes and puts them on a tray of meat and says: *Eat, Shoes! Eat!*
And Nasrudin takes his coat and puts it into a bowl of sauce and he says: *Savour the sauce, coat! Enjoy!*

Everybody is astonished. There is silence.
Then Amir says: *Nasrudin, my dearest friend, what are you doing?*

Nasrudin looks up and says:
*This evening when I came without my coat and hat and
my leather shoes, I was turned away from your gates.
But when I returned dressed in my coat and hat and
leather shoes, I was allowed in to your house. That
means it's not I who's invited to your dinner; it's
obvious it's the coat and the hat and the shoes that are
invited to your dinner. It is therefore that I bid them eat
for it is not I who's invited!*

And Amir embraces Nasrudin and says: *You are my true
friend, Nasrudin, for you point out to me the truths in
life.*

And Amir seats Nasrudin at the place of honor on his
right; and Amir offers Nasrudin fine clothes and many
gold coins but Nasrudin refuses them all for he has no
use for such things.

Amir then instructs all his guards and servants that
Nasrudin may from now come and go as he pleases, any
time and any day Nasrudin chooses to do so; no one is to
prevent Nasrudin from coming into Amir's home any
way he pleases.

Nasrudin back at home

After dinner, Nasrudin returns home and recounts the events to his donkey.
I refused all the clothes and gold he offered me,
Nasrudin says proudly to his donkey.

The donkey brays: *Hee-haw!Hee-haw!*
Oh, you're so disagreeable! says Nasrudin.

Nasrudin loses his donkey

Poor Nasrudin. He lost his donkey.

News traveled. Everyone heard about how poor
Nasrudin had lost his only donkey.
Some felt happy that misfortune had befallen Nasrudin.
After all, he was always laughing, wasn't he? Let him
cry for a change!

But some felt sorry for Nasrudin and so they came to see
Nasrudin at his home. Perhaps they could help him find
the donkey.
But when the crowd arrived at Nasrudin's home, they
were surprised to see Nasrudin smiling.
He seemed unusually happy for a man who had just lost
his only donkey.

Nasrudin, said one of men in the crowd. *We heard you
lost your donkey.*
Nasrudin laughed and he said, *Oh yes I've just lost my
donkey.*
And again Nasrudin laughed.

We are sorry to hear about that, said an old woman.
And another man shouted, quite displeased with
Nasrudin's smiles and laughter:
*We came here because we felt sorry for you, and we
want to help you look for the donkey. But you don't seem
sad that you've lost your donkey! If I were you, I'd be
real sad!*

Sad? shouted Nasrudin, laughing aloud. *Sad?* he said, again smiling. *Can't you see my good fortune? I'm happy that I wasn't riding that donkey – otherwise I'd be lost too*!

Nasrudin's gold coin

One morning, Nasrudin was counting his gold coins.
One of the gold coins rolled off the table, and down the
flight of steps that led directly to the street.

Nasrudin ran after the gold coin.
It jumped off each step and then rolled down to the
street.
Nasrudin followed carefully and quickly.

Nasrudin saw it roll through the narrow space below the
door of his store-room.

Nasrudin started to search for his gold coin on the
walkway.
He looked hard and he searched carefully.

Somebody stopped and said: *Nasrudin. What are you
looking for?*

My gold coin, said Nasrudin.

Hm, thought the man. *I'll pretend to help him and keep
the gold coin for myself if I do find it.*
And so now there were Nasrudin and the passer-by who
were looking for the gold coin.

Soon others joined in.

What are you looking for? a passer-by would ask.

Nasrudin's gold coin, someone would say.

And soon there were Nasrudin and a crowd looking for a gold coin that had been lost on the walkway.

Then the crowd grew tired of this search.

Are you sure, Nasrudin, an old woman shouted, *that the coin actually rolled down to the walkway? Did you actually see it?*

Everybody stopped searching and looked at Nasrudin.

Nasrudin said, *No, my gold coin rolled down below the door of my dark store-room here.*

And the man shouted: *You fool, Nasrudin. Why don't you look in the store-room rather than making us all look out in the street?*

You fool! said Nasrudin. *It's bright out here in the streets and dark in the store-room! How can we find it in the store-room where it's so dark? We got a better chance of finding it in the light, so continue with your search, you fools!*

Nasrudin dies

...yes, I was with him when he died...I had word he was not well, and I visited him and I was in the room where he died...

Nasrudin dies

Nasrudin is lying in his bed.

He is old. He is tired.
He is smiling. He is dying.

Donkey died some years ago.
And since donkey died, Nasrudin had walked. *There'll
never be a better donkey than Donkey,* Nasrudin would
say when anybody offered him a donkey for free.
Or if someone offered a donkey for sale. *Donkey nature
is rare,* he'd say.

And now Nasrudin lies dying. He is still smiling.
Ah, Death is here, he whispers. *Death is beautiful and
Death is here.*

And the women gather round Nasrudin.
They are dressed in their best clothes. They have their
finest jewelry on.

Someone whispers to Nasrudin: *They are here,
Nasrudin.*

Nasrudin opens his eyes. His smile disappears.

Dearest women, Nasrudin says. *What are you doing dressed in your finest clothes and looking so beautiful? Please go and dress like hags for I fear Death may find you more attractive a catch today than an old man like me ...*

And Nasrudin smiles. The women know the time has come.

It is beautiful, says Nasrudin. *Death too is beautiful.*

And Nasrudin dies.

And he dies as he smiles.